Born in 1972, Laurent Gaudé is one of France's most highly respected playwrights and novelists. He has won many prizes including the Goncourt in 2004 for *The Scortas' Sun*, published in 34 countries.

Emily Boyce is in-house translator and editor at Gallic Books.

Jane Aitken is a publisher and translator from the French.

Hell's Gate

Laurent Gaudé

Hell's Gate

Laurent Gaudé

Translated from the French by
Emily Boyce and Jane Aitken

Gallic Books
London

A Gallic Book

First published in France as *La porte des enfers* by Actes Sud, 2008
Copyright © Actes Sud, 2008

English translation copyright © Gallic Books, 2016
First published in Great Britain in 2016 by
Gallic Books, 59 Ebury Street,
London, SW1W 0NZ

A CIP record for this book is available from the British Library
ISBN 978-1-910477-32-8

Typeset in Fournier MT by Gallic Books
Printed in the UK by CPI (CR0 4YY)
2 4 6 8 10 9 7 5 3 1

For Anna
May the sound of your laughter be heard there
and bring comfort to those we miss

I
The Dead Rise Again
(August 2002)

For a long time, I called myself Filippo Scalfaro. Today I am taking my name back and saying it in full: Filippo Scalfaro De Nittis. When the sun came up this morning, I became older than my father. I stand at the kitchen window, waiting for the coffee to finish brewing. I have a stomach ache. No surprise – I have a long, hard day ahead of me. I've made myself an especially bitter coffee to keep me going – I'll be needing it. Just as the coffee pot starts to whistle on the stove, a plane takes off from Capodichino airport and the air begins to hum. I watch the plane's flat metal stomach rising up over the rooftops and I wonder what would happen if it dropped out of the sky onto the thousands of people below it – but it keeps soaring upwards, pulling free of its own weight. I turn off the heat on the stove and splash my face with water. My father. I'm thinking of him. This is his day. My father – whose face I can barely picture. The sound of his voice has gone completely. Sometimes I think I remember things he used to say – but whether he really said them or I've just made them up after all these years to fill the gap he left, I don't know. The only way I can really get close to him is by looking at myself in the mirror. There must be something of him there, in the shape of my eyes or the line of my cheekbones. From this day, when I look in the mirror I'll see the face he would have had if he'd had the chance to grow old. I carry my father within me.

This morning, at the first light of dawn, I felt him climb onto my shoulders like a child. He's counting on me now. Today's the day it will all happen. I've been working towards this for so long.

I sip my coffee slowly as the steam rises off it. I'm not afraid. I've already been to hell – what could possibly be scarier than that? All I have to ward off are my own nightmares. At night, the blood-curdling cries and groans of pain come flooding back. I smell the nauseating stench of sulphur. The forest of souls surrounds me. At night, I become a child again, begging the world not to swallow me up. I tremble from head to toe and I call out to my father. I scream, choke back tears, cry. Other people might call them nightmares, but they're wrong. If these were only dreams or visions, I'd have no reason to be afraid. But I know that what I see is real – I've been there. Nothing else frightens me. As long as I'm awake, I fear nothing.

The walls have stopped shaking from the roar of the jet engines. The only trace left in the sky is a long cotton-wool trail. I was planning to shave this morning, make a fresh start, but maybe I won't bother. No, wait, I must. I want to look as boyish as possible tonight. If there's a chance he might recognise me, I want to make sure he does. The water running into the sink is dirty, yellowish. My time is coming. I'll have my father with me. I've planned my revenge. I'm ready. Let the blood flow tonight. It feels right. I pull on a shirt to spare myself the sight of my skinny body. Naples is slowly waking up. Only slaves get up this early. I know this time of day well, when the ghosts loitering around the central station look for somewhere to hide their cardboard boxes.

I'll head into the city centre. I won't let my face give

anything away. I'll go into the restaurant through the service entrance as I have done every morning for the past two years. Ristorante Da Bersagliera. Via Partenope will be empty – no taxis, no Vespas. Boats will bob on the water at Santa Lucia. The grand seafront hotels will seem as quiet and still as majestic sleeping elephants. I'll get on with my shift and not let anything show until tonight. The coffee I made myself just now will see me through. I make coffee like nobody else. That's why, every evening at seven o'clock, I'm allowed to come out into the restaurant. I leave the washing up and trays of dirty water behind and take my place by the espresso machine. It's all I do. I don't take orders or carry any dishes. Most of the customers don't even see me. I make the coffees. But I've made a name for myself in Naples. Some people have even started coming especially because of me. I'll be in the restaurant this evening as usual, smiling away until it's time to take my revenge.

I head out of the door of my apartment. I won't be coming back. I take nothing with me. All I need are the car keys. I feel strong. I've come back from the dead. I have memories of hell and fears of the world ending. Today, I'll be reborn. My time has come. I close the door behind me. It's sunny outside. The planes will go on shaking the walls of Secondigliano. They all take off towards the sea, skimming over the buildings. I'm going to take my place at Da Bersagliera and wait for nightfall. I hope he'll be there. I'm not worried. My stomach isn't aching any more. I walk quickly. My father is with me now. Today is the day I take my name back and I say it once more in full: Filippo Scalfaro De Nittis.

Stay calm. Look bland and unremarkable. Nothing about the way I move or the expression on my face must give me away, no nervous twitching or sweating. I keep glancing at him out of the corner of my eye, but I can't stare straight at him as I wish I could. I knew he'd come. He's like clockwork – every Thursday night, he's here. Sometimes he brings a girl with him and she'll spend the night either laughing idiotically or pouting like an actress. Sometimes he eats alone, rushing to pay his bill and get back to the hotel where the girls are waiting for him. Tonight he's on his own. I saw him stride in the way he always does, as if he owns the place, knowing the staff will drop everything to serve him. He holds his arms out for them to take his coat and waits for a chair to be pulled out for him. He laps up the stares from the customers at nearby tables who wonder what he's done to deserve this five-star treatment when nothing about the way he looks, dresses or acts suggests he's anything special. He likes to be waited on.

My patience has paid off. I stayed in the kitchen for ages, hoping the boss would eventually put me on coffee duty. Time dragged on. I seemed to be constantly scrubbing the same plate, taking the same dishes out of the dishwasher. But when the first sitting moved on to dessert, I heard the boss barking at me to come out into the restaurant. I dried my hands on a cloth and told myself to seize the moment and make it go my way. I pulled off my white apron and took my place in front of the coffee machine.

The two American women on table 8 want cappuccinos with their pasta. The waiter has just passed on their order, sniffing at the sacrilege of it. I make the coffees as slowly as possible to give myself time to watch him. The noise of conversation rises, voices booming under the glass roof. The general havoc keeps my mind occupied. Waiters zip in and out of the kitchen, their footsteps gliding across the tiled floor. They hurry past without a glance in my direction, occasionally giving me an instruction through gritted teeth. Coffee on 7. I look down at my hands to check if they're shaking, but my body's calm. I must be paler than usual, but who's going to notice? The stomach pains are back, that's all, like distant twinges, reminders of a blow I was dealt a long time ago, a blow from which I've never recovered. The boss is coming over. Slowly. He says table 18 wants a word. I look up. It's the *ingegnere* on 18. I know what I have to do. The *ingegnere* is a regular. He's just finished his meal and wants to put my skills to the test. I go over to his table. He smiles at me. He says he's had a good meal and now he'd like a little coffee, but a proper one, none of this chlorinated decaffeinated stuff; he says he needs a good night's sleep, but can't stand the taste of decaf. He asks if I can do that for him. I nod. He gives me a wink. I can do anything, and he knows it. I go back to the machine. I'm the king of coffee. That's why I work here. A loser like me could never land a job like this otherwise. Nobody in Naples can claim to make better coffee than me. I get it from my father. Not my first father; the other one: Garibaldo Scalfaro. He got it from his uncle before him. Whatever you want, however you're feeling, I've got the coffee for it. Strong as a slap in the face to wake you up in the morning. Smooth and mellow to treat a headache. Silky and creamy to get you in the mood. Full-bodied and long-lasting to keep you awake. Coffee for biding your time. Coffee to make your blood boil. I measure out doses like an alchemist, using spices the palate won't notice but the body will recognise. The *ingegnere* on 18 will sleep well tonight and he won't have a heavy head in the morning. I smile. For the last few weeks, the owner has been itching to show off my talents. He's waiting for the new menus he's ordered with 'Da Bersagliera's Magic Coffee' printed on them. Your wish is our command ... And of course it's a chance for him to put prices up. Soon I'll be the star attraction ... I smile. It'll come to nothing. Tonight I'll be making my last coffee and handing it to the man I've had my eye on all night: Toto Cullaccio. And by the time the boss's shiny new menus arrive, I'll be long gone and he'll have to throw them away, cursing my name.

Toto Cullaccio, whom I'm no longer letting out of my sight, is finishing his plate of calamari. His shirt is stained with amatriciana sauce from the pasta course. Happens every time. He has slightly shaky hands and his fork slips out of his grasp. I thank God he hasn't died before now. Toto Cullaccio. To look at him, you'd think he'd retired from the post office. His hair's all fallen out, his fingers are puffy. But I know what he's capable of. I know why he walks around like he owns the place and why, when he waves me over irritably, he does it not like a customer to a waiter, but like a master to his dog.

I put my cloth down behind the counter and walk towards him. As I draw nearer, he gestures to me to bend down so he can speak into my ear, and his dirty voice whispers that the night isn't over yet, he has two pretty girls to go back to, the expensive kind, but he hasn't got the energy he used to, especially after the meal he's just had. He murmurs that he's not worried, because he knows I can make him a little coffee to help him put on a good show. He doesn't wait for me to answer. He knows it can be done. I go back to my machine. I can feel my heart racing. I'm starting to sweat. Blood is pumping through my temples. Now I'm dripping with sweat. My guts are wrenching. I feel like I'm bleeding again. I need to stay strong. I'm a child crouching on the ground. I can hear my father's voice sounding further and further away. I have to get a grip on myself, not let visions and fears get the better of me. Tonight's the night. Now. In a few seconds. My father is thirsty for it. He's calling out to me. The last drops of coffee run into the cup. I haven't added anything to it. No matter. It'll have no special properties but Toto Cullaccio won't be drinking it anyway. I place the cup and saucer on the tray. I put a knife there too. I walk towards Toto Cullaccio. The room is hot. As I pass a table, I almost knock over a jug of water. I feel pangs in my stomach. I'm very close to him now. Before he senses me behind him, I say his name loud and clear, I say 'Toto Cullaccio' and he jumps. The customers sitting nearby go quiet because I've said his name so forcefully and I am standing here, pale and still, for no apparent reason. He has turned to glare at me. I meet his gaze. It's him. Here we are again. So I carry on; I tell him my name is Pippo De Nittis, and it feels strange. I say it loudly; the whole restaurant hears. Heads turn, conversations stop. He's about to ask me what I want and how I've dared to call him by his name and tell him mine – which he really couldn't give a damn about – but I cut him off. I let go of the tray, so that the coffee, the glass of water, everything, goes crashing around my feet, and I plant the knife in his stomach. Screams ring out around us. Everything becomes still. People are rooted to the spot, their mouths hanging open in shock. I like the silence around me. I want them all to see me, so that they can tell everyone what they saw. I was careful not to push the knife in to the hilt. I don't want to kill him – I want to hurt him, make him moan and cry, not spill his guts all over the table. Moving quickly, I step behind Cullaccio and slip the knife under his throat. Everything happens in fast-forward. My stomach no longer hurts. I can hear everything, see everything. The women can't take in what they're witnessing. The men can't bring themselves to stand, they're so scared. Cullaccio begins to scream in pain. His shirt is already spattered with blood. Simply by pressing a blade to his flesh, I force him out of his chair. His stomach must be killing him, but he gets to his feet. I knock over a couple of tables on the way to the door. Nobody thinks of stopping us. Cullaccio is yelping like a dog. I know what it's like. I cried too, all those years ago, bent double, clutching my stomach, unable to breathe. I was a child then. He's forgotten all of that. It's fine. He has all the time in the world to remember.

We leave the restaurant and the harbour air rushes into my veins. The silence of the boats at Santa Lucia is broken by our passing. The car is waiting for us. The hardest part is climbing the steps to Via Partenope. I hear him groan with every movement he makes. Lumbering along like a whale, Cullaccio limps, sobs, implores me, I think, but I take no notice. My knife landed perfectly – I left him with the strength to walk; he hasn't passed out. Here we are. I tell him to open the car door and I throw him into the passenger seat. He curls up like a snail, finally able to lick his wounds. I hear him crying as he clutches his belly. He's getting blood all over the seat. I make my way quickly round to the other side of the car, still holding the knife in my hand. I get in next to him and slam my own door closed. It's a beautiful night, humid and calm. I feel good. We have all the time in the world.

II
Death on Via Forcella
(June 1980)

Matteo De Nittis began to walk even faster. Little Pippo had trouble keeping up but didn't dare say anything. His father was holding him by the hand and tugged him along each time he slowed down. They were already half an hour late and Matteo knew they wouldn't be there for at least another ten minutes. They made their way along Via Nolana, dodging the people lingering in front of the stalls. Occasionally Matteo knocked into someone and barely bothered to apologise. He was muttering to himself through clenched teeth, cursing the people blocking his way, the never-ending streets and this day that had started so badly.

Giuliana had had to go to the hotel earlier than usual. Two of her colleagues were away, and it had been agreed that she would cover for them. She had left her husband to take their little boy to school. As she drank her coffee in the kitchens of the Grand Hotel Santa Lucia with her bleary-eyed colleagues, she tried to imagine how the two men in her life were getting on, what they were saying to each other. She felt comforted at the thought of them together. Father and son. Then it was time for her to go upstairs and begin the day's work, leaving behind her cup, still steaming with the remains of her coffee. And leaving behind too the thought of her husband and son and her longing to see them again. She determined not to think of them any more, and busied herself with her work.

Matteo and Pippo were both sweating. They had spent an hour stuck in traffic before finally reaching Porta Nolana. Naples had become a giant knot of stationary cars exuding petrol fumes and irritation. Matteo had been beside himself with impatience, drumming his hands on the steering wheel. Earlier that morning he had had to take a passenger to the airport and there was no choice but to take Pippo with him. On the way back the traffic had snarled up disastrously. Every route was blocked. After an hour, since the roads were still in chaos, Matteo had decided to park the car and continue on foot. 'It will be quicker,' he had said. But it was market day and the crowds pressing round him seemed to be there simply to take over from the traffic and to ensure that the rest of the journey was just as exhausting.

Now he was practically running. Pippo was red in the face, not because he was having to walk so quickly, but because his father had just lost his temper with him. The child had asked if he could stop for five minutes and Matteo had shouted no, they would stop when they reached school and not a moment before, and Pippo was to keep quiet, to keep quiet and hurry up.

They were still running. Matteo continued to rant at everyone he bumped into, at every road they had to cross, at every Vespa that sped past, almost knocking them down. Faster. That was all he had in mind. To go faster and be done with this disastrous morning. To drop Pippo off, even though he was late, and in tears. To drop him off and finally draw breath. Once that was done, he would go and have a restorative coffee and splash some water on his face. He would dry his hands, and as he did so, the tension that had built up in the car and then during the dash through the crowded streets would slip away. Yes, he would have all the time in the world to compose himself and cool down. But right now it was getting later and later by the second and it was torture.

It had been some time since Giuliana had last worked upstairs, cleaning the guest rooms, with her back bent and using quick, efficient movements. She usually worked on the ground floor, helping with breakfast in the dining room. She laid tables, took drinks orders from the guests and made sure they had everything they wanted. For three hours, guests came and went. They arrived looking sleepy or pressed for time, but all filled with the same desire to be fed and to come to gradually, surrounded by the reviving smell of coffee. She filled plates, removed dirty tablecloths and made sure the hot water urn was never empty. She enjoyed herself. As she moved from table to table she heard all the languages of the world being spoken. No one paid any attention to her. She went discreetly about the dining room, alert to the guests' needs.

Today, working along the second-floor corridor, she was engulfed in silence and the aroma of coffee did not reach her. She was alone. It was like starting out again. It was here she had begun working five years ago as a cleaner. She remembered the long, silent carpeted corridors. You had to go into every room and do exactly the same thing in each one, the same cleaning ritual: open the window, plump up the pillows, make the bed, change the towels, clean the bathroom, then hoover. There she was, outside room 205, knowing that she had a long morning of housekeeping in front of her. She smiled. She had just remembered the two nights she had spent here, at the Grand Hotel Santa Lucia. Twice she had been the one slipping into the luxurious rooms. When Giosuè at reception had let her know at the last minute about very late cancellations. Rooms that had been paid for but were empty. They had leapt at the chance, she and Matteo. That had been before Pippo was born. Two nights. In a beautiful luxury hotel. She smiled. Remembering the pleasure of those two nights made her day's work seem bearable.

As they turned into Vicolo della Pace, Matteo felt a sense of relief. The street was less crowded. The market was ending so there would be far fewer people to get in their way. Just then the little boy began to cry. He said he was tired, his father was hurting his arm, his lace was undone and he wanted to stop. Matteo didn't listen. He continued to pull his son along, saying angrily, 'Hurry up,' so that the child would realise that until they reached the school gate, he shouldn't ask anything; in fact, shouldn't say anything at all, just grit his teeth and follow.

Matteo hesitated for a fraction of a second to decide which side of the road to take. He would have preferred to walk in the shade, but that would mean crossing over, which would use up more time, so he decided to press on in the sun. He was already streaming with sweat anyway.

That was where, at the corner of Vicolo della Pace and Via Forcella, the world fell apart. At first he didn't notice anything. He pulled on the child's arm with the same insistence. When passers-by began to scream, he stopped. He wasn't worried. He didn't understand what was happening. He looked around. Everything had become strange. Everywhere, he saw faces with mouths wide open. He heard shouts; a woman with a wicker bag was a few feet in front of him on all fours by a car, waving her feet as if a spider were crawling up them. He stood still for what seemed like an eternity, then his body appeared to register what was happening and he threw himself to the ground. Fear paralysed his muscles, his mind, his breathing. He heard gunshots. Then several more in response. He had pulled his son down and held him tightly. He could smell the tar warmed by the morning sun. Shouts came from all around. There were long shrill moans from people trying to expel their fear and breathe again.

He hugged Pippo with all his might. The embrace was the only thing that mattered in that moment. It helped him think straight. He tried to analyse the situation. He was in the middle of the street, caught in a shoot-out. The sound of glass breaking erupted a few feet away, setting off several car alarms. The best plan was not to move until everything stopped. To wait. To wait for the police, the emergency services and for silence to return. To wait until he could stand up again. He was winded. The blood throbbed in his temples. He stayed like that, lying down, his hand on his son's head. The seconds ticked past with painful slowness. He no longer paid attention to the noise around him. He was praying, saying 'Hail Mary' over and over again.

Then slowly silence did return.

A telephone started to ring in one of the rooms on the second floor. The ringing reverberated along the corridors of the Grand Hotel Santa Lucia. At first she paid no attention. She was in room 209. A group had left early that morning, freeing up the ten rooms on the corridor. She had to do them all. The door to 209 was open. She was on her knees, wiping the bathroom floor with a cloth, and did not get up. The telephone rang on. After a while, she put the cloth down, wiped her hands and walked out of 209 and into the corridor. She couldn't tell which room the ringing telephone was in. She moved along the corridor, trying to work out where the noise was coming from. The telephone was still ringing. Finally, she found the room and went in, approaching the phone with the trepidation of someone who knows that tragedy awaits them.

Matteo was unsure how much time had elapsed. Voices still reverberated around him, but they no longer sounded panicked. The voices were asking if everything was all right, if anyone had been hurt, if someone had called the police. Matteo felt relief when he heard the police siren – far away at first, but getting closer all the time.

He released his grasp. The danger had passed. He began to tremble uncontrollably. His fear left him. How late would they be now? The thought was laughable. None of that mattered any more. He stroked his son's back, telling him that it was over, that he could stand up now, that the danger was gone. The little boy didn't move.

Pippo? The child didn't reply. The colour drained from Matteo's face. He knelt down. His shirt was soaked with blood. Pippo? He couldn't breathe. His son wasn't moving; he was lying face down on the ground, inert. Pippo? He shouted. He didn't know what to do. He shouted again. Because he didn't know how to stop the blood he loved so much from spreading over the pavement. His hands were running all over his son's body, as if trying, unsuccessfully, to find the wound and stop it bleeding. His hands were all red, slippery, bathed in blood and seemed totally useless: he did not know what he should be doing with them.

People came over looking anxious. They stood a few feet away, repeating that an ambulance was on its way, but he could barely hear them. He was concentrating on not crying. More people gathered, but did nothing. He shouted out. That someone should go for help. That they should hurry. No one moved. Everything was unbearably slow.

She had just hung up. She sat on the bed she had made a little earlier, alone in a too-clean room. She was nothing but a void. She was nowhere and felt nothing. The day had just imploded. She could not move. She did not cry out, or get up and run. The people on the floor below, and in the neighbouring rooms, or people anywhere did not know that she was in that room, in a state of nothingness. She did not move from the too-soft bed, convinced that her life had stopped, and that from now on everything was meaningless.

In Via Forcella, men in uniform at last appeared through the crowd and came to kneel beside Matteo. He asked them to save his son. He did not want to let go of Pippo's head, which was like a dead weight in his hands. But that wasn't possible. Not his son. Not today. Someone helped him up. The ambulance men had brought a stretcher; he had to let them through and leave them to their work.

Someone was asking him questions. His name, his address. He tried to listen to what they were saying, but couldn't really follow. He registered on the faces of the people around him the gravity of his situation. He did not want to let go of Pippo's hand. Even though it was cold and lifeless, that was all he asked. To keep hold of his son's hand. They could take him wherever they wanted, as long as they did not ask him to let go. They seemed to sense he would not, and let him be. They opened the ambulance doors and he was able to get in behind the stretcher.

Pippo and he were huddled together in the midst of blankets and boxes of dressings. The engine started up. How many times had he seen ambulances in Naples? How many times had he pulled over to let one overtake him? Now he was inside. He didn't know where they were going. The important thing was to find somewhere Pippo could be treated. That was the only thing that mattered. In the ambulance they put a tube in Pippo's mouth. He found that strangely comforting. It meant there were things they could do, actions they could perform, protocols to be followed. They were going to do what they were best at. It would perhaps be long and painful; there might be hours, if not days, of worry, but it didn't matter, he would never give up. He had decided his son would survive this day. Matteo would rescue him from this street, from the inquisitive passers-by and from this ambulance that smelt of blood and dressings.

The ambulance stopped. He waited a few seconds, and then the back doors opened and he was blinded by the light.

He stepped out of the ambulance. They were in the inner courtyard of a hospital. He looked around for the emergency entrance and that's when he saw her. She was coming towards them. He didn't immediately grasp why she was there. Giuliana? She didn't reply. He wanted to ask her how she knew, who had told her they were coming here. He didn't remember that he was the one who had given the police his wife's name and the number they could reach her on. 'Giuliana. Listen …' He held his arms out to her, but it wasn't him Giuliana was walking to. 'Giuliana, you have to be strong …' She paid no attention to him. She was marching straight over to the ambulance. Her face was contorted, her nose running, her mouth twisted. She said nothing. As she passed, he tried to stop her. He wanted her to come to him so that he could take her in his arms. He wanted to tell her to stay calm. That he knew what had happened back there. He also wanted someone to explain to them what the doctors were going to do for Pippo. But Giuliana ignored him. She didn't even see him. None of the men standing round the vehicle, ambulance men and police, dared to stop her. She went into the back of the ambulance and they all heard her start to moan.

Something was odd. He was about to join her in the ambulance, but he stayed where he was, quite still, trying to figure out what was strange. And then, gradually, it started to dawn on him, becoming more and more obvious: she knew. Giuliana knew something he didn't. Perhaps the ambulance staff had told her when they rang to ask her to come quickly, perhaps she just knew with a mother's intuition, at the very moment it happened. But he knew now, too – Pippo was dead. That was how he found out. Watching Giuliana. It must be true otherwise why was no one moving? Why were they not taking Pippo into the hospital, yelling orders so as not to lose a moment? Why would they leave a mother wailing in the ambulance, instead of telling her to be brave and that they would do everything they could to save her son?

That was how he realised. And there was nothing else he could do but stand there, useless and defeated, in the midst of these men who lowered their eyes out of embarrassment and pity. He should never have let go of Pippo's hand. That was what he was thinking. Not let go of his hand. Ever. As long as he was holding it, Pippo was alive. He had had to let go to get out of the ambulance. So he wanted to get back into the ambulance and take his hand again and continue holding it. He took two steps towards the vehicle, but two men prevented him from going further. They did it kindly, looking sad and apologetic, although they said nothing. Who were they? Why were they not letting him through? Why could he not go and be with his son again? Was that what was troubling them? He had to get back into the ambulance. His son needed him. Was that a problem for them?

They held him back gently but firmly. The idea crossed his mind that they were there to explain to him. They were letting him know that he would never be able to hug his little boy, or touch him, or kiss him, or ruffle his hair. He wouldn't be able to do that any more. They were separated. He and his son. That was what he had to understand. His son, Pippo, whom he would never see again, never touch, whose forehead he would never again kiss, his son who had been snatched from him in a second. He would never be able to cuddle him. Ever again. His son. Then his legs gave way and he fell to the ground.

III
Kneeling on My Tomb
(August 2002)

I start the car, screeching away from the kerb. Cullaccio is still groaning in the seat next to me. He can't take it all in. This is not the evening he had planned. Everything can change in the space of a split second – I should know. The life you imagined turns to dust and you're left with nothing but a pain that won't go away. He's gasping for air, bleeding heavily in his chair. He needn't worry – he won't die of his injury. I made sure I didn't pierce his stomach. The blood is running, soaking through the crotch of his trousers. He's afraid. I know how that feels. He can see himself dying here after hours of suffering. I know how that feels too.

We drive on. I know the way by heart – I've rehearsed this so many times. I glide along Via Partenope, following the seafront. The cobbles jolt us up and down in our seats. With every bump, he groans a little louder. We head down towards the port. He doesn't ask questions, just grumbles, whimpers and talks rubbish. Maybe he thinks I'm going to hit him. What would be the point? He's already in pain. The road is covered in potholes – that's torture enough. I make no effort to avoid them. He clings to the glovebox and tries to catch his breath, but soon he's wriggling like an eel again. He can't find a comfortable position. I've been there too. I remember squirming, trying to push the pain out of my body, but it was no good. It was a long struggle for me, too, with my father screaming and crying next to me. I remember how white my father's face was, how he could do nothing but hold me tightly, so I would at least feel the comfort of his arms.

I wonder if Cullaccio's blood is dripping from the car. I'd have to pull over to check. It would be good if it was – I'd like to see his blood spilt on the streets of Naples, for it to soak through the tarmac and wake my father. It's dark now. The buildings to our left are as gloomy as a town abandoned to the plague. The lights from the handful of cargo ships docked on our right are reflected on Cullaccio's sweat-covered face. He looks like a crying clown. No one will hear him whining. Even if they did, people keep themselves to themselves around here. I try not to drive too fast. I want to make the most of this. I hear his gurgles of pain and every so often catch him grimacing. This is good.

We pass the two turrets overlooking Piazza del Carmine. This is where I was born. I tell him so. He says nothing in reply. I don't know if he heard me or realised I was talking to him, so I tell him again: here, right there, on the lawn at the foot of the turrets. He stares back wide-eyed. He looks more scared than if I'd just told him I was about to give him a beating. I must be mad. That's the only possible explanation. Nobody's born here, beneath the turrets opposite the harbour. It's just a patch of dirty grass strewn with beer cans, where junkies and illegal immigrants sleep, lulled by the constant drone of traffic. But I'm not lying – this really was where I came into the world for the second time. Of course, the first time I was born it was in a hospital, coming out of my mother's belly, surrounded by her visceral warmth. But years later, I was born again here, purely by my father's will. The air I breathed in was the air of this filthy dual carriageway and, as at my first birth, I blinked in amazement and screamed as the oxygen burnt through my lungs. I remember it all. Even what came before, which makes me sick and fills my head with screams at night. But I won't tell him about that. There's too much to say. Maybe in time he'll work out who I am. He won't understand – who could? – but the goose pimples and shivers running over his skin will tell him everything I'm holding back. For now, he's trying his luck, doing his best to talk through the pain. I'm not listening. He must have decided to try to reason with me. Maybe he's offering me money, or begging me for mercy. He keeps on talking, but I'm miles away. I'm remembering my mother's eyes, the deep warmth of her neck. That was so long ago. I remember her smell and her infectious laugh. My mother, who turned her back on me. Dropped me, like a memory she would rather forget.

We pass the outlines of two black steel silos on our left. Only the shells of the huge cylinders remain, but they loom, redundant, over the surrounding buildings. Soon I'll have to move into the right-hand lane and leave Naples by the *tangenziale*.

When I indicate to join the motorway, Cullaccio begins to panic. He's like a spider caught in a torch beam. He can't bear the idea of being torn away from the backstreets of Naples. I'm going fast now. The *tangenziale* rises above the city. We pass the business quarter, its five or six tightly packed skyscrapers rising up out of nowhere like a forest of money amid the grime. The road signs point to Bari or the Amalfi Coast. I change lanes. It's a maze of bridges, roads, entrances and exits. Capodichino. I follow signs for the airport. A plane takes off in the darkness and passes overhead. I imagine how the passengers would react if the pilot told them the car they'd just flown over contained a man in his sixties bleeding his guts out like a pig. Up above us or driving down the opposite carriageway, people pass by, totally unaware of what's happening. So many lives sliding past, oblivious to one another.

Cullaccio is panicking. His pain is giving way to terror. He's noticed the signs for the airport and he thinks I'm going to make him board a plane. To where? If I told him where I've come from, he'd be begging for God's mercy. I leave the *tangenziale*. We drive alongside the cemetery, looking down over the city. He thinks – I can tell from the pitiful expression on his face – that I'm looking for a place to kill him. I pass the main gate of the cemetery. I don't stop. I need to go a bit further. Three hundred yards on there's another entrance, smaller and less frequently used. I park in front of the rusty old gate. I've often come here at night and imagined what this day would be like.

I drag Cullaccio out of his seat. He falls to the ground and lies there for a while, crying like an old woman, face covered in snot, legs bathed in blood. I leave him there – there's no risk of him getting away. I fetch a pair of bolt cutters from the boot and slice through the padlock. The gate is stiff, rusted to the ground by years of neglect. I rattle it angrily. It gives way, opening just enough to let us through. Cullaccio's going to have to stand up now. I tell him so, my voice sufficiently authoritative that he gets to his feet, weak as he is. We enter the cemetery. The gravestones look like strange ships in the night. I mustn't be afraid. Mustn't let the nightmares take hold of me. The statues seem to smile at us as we pass. I recognise the heavy silence of death. I begin to struggle for breath. I need to focus on Cullaccio and forget everything else. We walk between the rows, scattering several cats as we go. I push him ahead of me. He stumbles often. It's good to see. The living sound of him struggling to walk brings me comfort. It really is him, in the flesh, carrying his pain and his injury. Each time he falls I hoist him back up and push him in front of me again. He's puffing like an animal. It's strange how little I feel. I don't take my eyes off him but I feel no pity, no disgust, in spite of his ugly, childish cries.

'There it is.' The sound of my voice stops him in his tracks, like an order. He turns and scours the area around us. I point to a gravestone. There it is. I want him on his knees. He turns his head towards me. He looks like a gargoyle, pleading. He starts to speak, stammers that he doesn't know who I am but if he's done something to upset me … I don't let him finish. We're here. I show him the headstone and ask him to read it. He turns his head anxiously. 'Out loud,' I add. I want to hear him say it, loud and clear. He hesitates. I give him a kick, the way you nudge a dog to make it run. He does as he's told. Filippo De Nittis. 1974–1980. His words turn to sobs. He doesn't know why he's crying: anticipating the blow he thinks is imminent, perhaps … He's racking his brains, but nothing comes to mind. The names and dates on the headstone are no help. He'd like to know who I am and what it is I want revenge for, but he doesn't dare ask me anything. At this point, I start to see things. I remember the Underworld. The vast, empty halls filled only with the wails of departed souls. The forest of ghouls where the trees are twisted by icy winds. I remember loose groups of souls walking together, waving the stumps of their limbs. All of this runs through my mind, roars in my ears. I have to stay strong. I think of my father again. I can feel him watching me, willing me on, bringing me to life. I take Cullaccio by the hair and push his face into the gravestone. I order him to put his hands on it. I can tell by his silence that he thinks this is it: I'm about to kill him. I pin him down by putting my knee on his head. His cheek must be rubbing against the granite. I grab hold of his wrist. With my right hand, I take the knife out of my pocket and I cut off his fingers. One swift action severs all but the thumb. As I cut, his whole body responds with a movement that almost throws me off. Blood pours from his mutilated hand. 'The other one.' I shout so he'll hear me despite the pain. He begs me to stop. I'm not listening. I take hold of his right hand and I look at it. That finger, his index finger – that's the one he shot with. The pressure on the metal trigger came from this finger. I start cutting again. The screams coming out of his mouth are horrendous. I get up. He collapses, sprawled on the tomb, clutching his two useless stumps to his belly. This is what I want – for him to stay this way for the rest of his life, powerless, unable to hold anything or perform the most basic tasks. He'll have to rely on people. He'll understand the humiliation of having to ask for help to get up, to brush his hair, blow his nose. A nurse will look after him like a poor old thing, doing her best to hide her disgust. He'll remember me with every simple gesture he can no longer make. I'll be with him until his dying day. I'll drive him mad. And if he tries to come after me, even if he puts the whole of Naples onto me, he'll soon find that all paths lead here, to the tomb he's howling on. Every time, he'll come up against a crazy truth he will never make sense of: my name is Pippo De Nittis and I died in 1980.

I leave him there, slumped on the ground, wailing, half conscious, muttering gibberish. I begin to walk away, retracing my steps back to the car. I take one last look at the scene to sear it onto my memory: the tombstone is spattered with blood. There are some fingers lying on it and others strewn on the ground around it. I bend down and pick up two fingers and then I leave Cullaccio to his pain. He won't die of this. He'll soon be found. He'll be carried off and treated and then they'll start asking questions. The customers at Da Bersagliera will have long since raised the alarm. It's fine. He isn't meant to die. I turn my back on him. I'm done with him. It's a mild night. The blood is pumping through my veins. I'll head back to the car and I'll go. There's still so much I need to do.

IV
The Lonely Road
(September 1980)

What happened afterwards, Matteo and Giuliana couldn't remember. Surely hours went by, one after another. Days too. But they felt as if life went on without them. Did they manage to sleep during that time? They must have, otherwise they would not have survived, but they didn't remember doing so. And, in fact, the idea of sleep seemed incongruous. There was no respite from the pain. They were living just one long day, made up of the same words said to them with that mixture of embarrassment and emotion. Friends, colleagues from the taxi office, neighbours, all spoke the same phrases, in low voices without waiting to hear the reply, as though placing an offering at the foot of a statue. Matteo and Giuliana said thank you. They said that they were touched. Or they said nothing, determined not to cry.

Frequently people congratulated Matteo on his courage. They thought he was strong and resilient. He always found that absurd because he knew he had been broken, he was destroyed. He was aware of all the things he could no longer do: enter Pippo's bedroom, say his name, go back to the places they used to go to together. He knew that he was in a perpetual state of stupor and that nothing mattered any more.

The hardest thing was hearing the shouts of children in the street. Especially when the children were the same age as Pippo, expressing the same delight at running behind a bike, or joyfully calling out to their neighbourhood friends. He heard them as he passed, '*Eh Anto', vieni qua!*' He shuddered. '*Ant', vieni a giocare.*' These were living children, he thought, hurrying on. They are all living, except mine. They went on as normal: racing about, playing catch. 'Anto'!' Perhaps they had played with his son. He didn't want to look at them because he knew what he would think: he wouldn't be able to stop himself cursing them. He would think, let death take one of them, never mind which one, one who would never amount to anything, or even all of them. He didn't care how many of them death took as long as it gave him his child back. Why were they still living? Were they better than Pippo? He hurried on, so that he would not grab them roughly by the sleeve and ask them, 'Why? Why?' like a madman.

Giuliana always wore the same expression now. Ashen and hollow-eyed, she spent most of her time sitting in an armchair, crying and desolate, like a faded photo of her previous self. One day – some time after Pippo's death – she got up and went out. She wanted to go to the cemetery. She hadn't been back there since the burial. She walked slowly to the bus stop. She waited, with a blank gaze holding her bag tightly under her arm. When the bus arrived, she didn't manage to get on. There it was in front of her, but her muscles wouldn't obey her. The driver waited a few seconds to see whether she would make up her mind, then he closed the doors again and drove off. She stayed rooted to the spot, still blank. She hadn't moved a muscle. Her body had not been able to respond. Eventually she set off on her way home, but very slowly, as though defeated by her own weakness.

*

Matteo did not tell anyone, even Giuliana, that he relived that terrible day over and over again. He was always in the same place at the corner of Via Forcella and Vicolo della Pace. He could not tear himself away from that pavement. He spent hours there in his thoughts. He continually went over the day. The day as it had happened, the day as it could have happened, the minute microscopic changes that could have altered the course of events. If he had walked a little less quickly. If he had not parked the car so that they could finish the journey on foot, or if he had parked somewhere else. If he had only crossed the road into the shade, which had occurred to him, or if he had taken the time to kneel down and re-tie Pippo's lace as the boy had asked … A few seconds at every stage would have been sufficient to ensure that they were a few inches out of harm's way. A few seconds earlier or later and the trajectory of the bullet would have missed the boy. A tiny thing, like hearing a voice he thought he knew, making him stop for a moment, or a Vespa roaring past that would have forced them to step back. But no. Everything had conspired to create that terrible conjunction of body and bullet. What force could have willed that? What horrible turn of fate had ensured that everything came together in that way? Was that what was known as the evil eye? And if it was, why had it chosen them that day? By chance or design?

At night, or when he was alone, he relived the sound of his son crying. He was there, holding his father's hand, whimpering because he had run so much and was tired of being dragged along. That was how they had parted: in anger. And he couldn't tell that to anyone, not even Giuliana. What on earth had made him so angry that he had hurried them into the path of death? Fear of being late for school? How petty and stupid that now seemed. If he had at least been able to talk to his son, in the street, or the ambulance, and tell him that he was there and loved him, and wasn't angry, but he hadn't said any of that. Pippo had died in the silence of his father's anger.

It took him a while to gather the strength to get his car back. When he finally decided to go, he went at night. He did not want the streets to have the feel of the day of the shooting. He did not want crowds, or noises, or the light to remind him of that day. He saw the car from afar. It was still there. He went over, opened the door and got in, his jaw clenched, and drove off. He did not pick up any passengers that night. He did not switch on the light that indicated whether he was available for hire or not. He wasn't in his car for work. He was just driving. He went from Capodichino airport to Santa Lucia, from Piazza Dante to the business district and from the port to Vomero. He drove without knowing why he was driving, sometimes stopping for several minutes at the side of the road, his hands trembling, his lips parted, his head bent. He drove until he was exhausted and only then did he resign himself to going home.

When he went into the bedroom, moving as quietly as possible because it was five in the morning, Giuliana turned over in bed without completely waking up and asked him, 'Have you started working again?' He did not reply. A few seconds passed during which he remained standing close to the bed, then she said, 'That's good,' before burying her head in the pillow, a sign that she wouldn't be speaking again. He said nothing. He did not contradict her. He did not explain anything about where he had been. He slipped into bed, letting her fall back to sleep with the comforting sense that her husband was a brave man slowly getting back to normal, a man she'd be able to rely on.

He, on the other hand, could not get to sleep. He thought back over his long nocturnal drive, from Mergellina to the station, along wide empty streets. He asked himself what he had been doing there, what hurt or desire had he been trying to assuage? Was he recovering as Giuliana thought or was he dropping into the abyss? He wondered if he would do it again, if he would go out like that every night like a man who wasn't seeking anything but who just wanted the soft night air to bathe his face.

Giuliana made another attempt to go to the cemetery. The idea haunted her. There was something there she had to overcome. The second time she did manage to board the bus. She was white-faced and kept her head down throughout the journey so that no one would ask her if she was all right or if she needed any help. She braced herself. The drive up to Santa Maria del Pianto seemed endless. The bus stopped in the traffic then jerked forward in fits and starts. She felt sick.

When she finally got off, the fresh air did her good. She walked slowly, gradually regaining her breath. Then she was outside the tall gates of the cemetery and stopped. She gazed at the wrought iron and the tombstones behind and decided not to go any further. She had failed again. She did not have the strength yet. She would have to overcome her reluctance over several attempts. She stared for a long time at the gates and then turned away. But this time she didn't feel undone. She knew she would succeed, but she wanted to do it in her own time. She wanted to be able to enter the cemetery without flinching or lowering her head, to do what she had decided to do there.

*

Matteo never worked in daytime again. Every evening he would leave the apartment at about six o'clock, only returning in the very early morning. It soothed him to be out at night behind his steering wheel. The world asked nothing of him, did not see him. He glided along, silent and miserable, and gave himself over to his grief. For several hours, he managed to forget everything and it was a profound relief. As he drove along deserted streets, catching sight of figures disappearing round corners, he found beauty in the grimy city. The people he saw, at those improbable hours, when the sky was darker than the road, were people he recognised. They were broken men, who were fleeing life or who had been rejected by it. He saw them – as he drove with all his windows down – drunk and pissing on the dirty pavement. 'Are they still living?' he wondered. 'They're shadows going from one place to another. Like me. With no substance. Trying to work out what to do with themselves. They're empty and floating. What do they still feel?' He saw them in the street – distraught, cut off in their solitude, their gaze vacant, wandering from one place to another, just for the sake of walking, so that they would not be on their own and tempted to end it all. He saw them, sometimes arguing, with the heavy slowness of drunkards or the dangerous swiftness of murderers. The people that the light of day chased away were there; he saw them roaming about filled with despair or spite.

He drove around at that strange hour when shops are no more than sad façades behind iron grilles, and when there was nothing that could remind him of the man he had once been. He drove, counting the beggars and the overturned dustbins. When he had no passengers, he turned off his engine wherever he was, in the port, near the station, in Via Partenope across the bay from Castel dell'Ovo, or in the grim little streets of the Spanish quarter. He let the sounds of the city wash over him as his thoughts wandered: why could men not just die away like flames? Just gently exhaust themselves until they were extinguished? That's what he would have liked for himself – it seemed to him to correspond to his real state. He should not continue, he should just gradually diminish, with ever shorter breaths, and eventually disappear. But that didn't happen and each evening, as the humid sea air swept through the empty Naples streets, he was forced to admit that he was still alive.

And then came that morning in September. Giuliana left the apartment with a determination she would not have believed herself capable of any more. The sun was rising and the façades of the buildings were half in shade and half in light. She had told the hotel the day before that she would not be going in, but had said nothing to Matteo because she wanted to be able to leave at her usual early time without having to explain. She walked all along Via Foria. She was pale and drawn but had a quiet strength about her. She knew that this was the day she would succeed. She did not want to take the bus. She wanted to walk. To get there by putting one foot in front of the other. She wanted to have time to think and to feel her fatigue pull on her muscles. She made her way to the Naples cemetery, up there on the heights of Santa Maria del Pianto, leaving the city behind to wake up in a halo of bluish pink.

She passed under the cemetery portal without hesitating. She walked through the tombs without flinching. When she arrived at her son's grave, she stopped dead and read the inscription without betraying any emotion.

'A stone, so that's all that remains of my son,' she said to herself. The silence all around was soothing. It would have been unbearable to meet other visitors or to be disturbed by the comings and goings of municipal employees. She was very still, not looking any more either at the stone or at the name engraved on it. On the horizon, the Bay of Naples sparkled like the scales of a fish. She was lost in memory. She could clearly recall the voices of those who had come to Pippo's funeral a few weeks earlier. She remembered walking behind the hearse, and the long ceremony during which she had held on to Matteo's arm to stop herself collapsing. She remembered the procession of people who all said the same thing. It was as if she was once again in the midst of the slow crowd walking behind the coffin. The empty cemetery seemed suddenly full of people again. She felt they were there in front of her. They were all there, around her, looking sombre in their black clothes. Family, friends, the local shopkeepers. Everyone. She felt a cold anger developing, an anger that could burn everything, destroy everything, the anger of grieving mothers who won't resign themselves. So she began speaking, right there in the middle of nowhere, at that hour of the day with only the birds to hear her and this was Giuliana's first curse:

'I curse you all, every one of you. For the world is ugly and it's you who have made it that way. You crowded round me, you smothered me with gentle words and solicitude but I did not want any of it. I curse the people who work in this cemetery who carried my son's coffin, relieved because they could not help noticing how light it was and how that was less tiring for them. I know that's what they were thinking even though it didn't show on their faces and I curse them for their thoughts.

'I curse the people who were there in the crowd, and whom I didn't know. They came out of malicious curiosity and I hope that one day they will cry for someone they love. I also curse our friends and their honest tears. I spit on any pain that is not mine and trample it underfoot. There is no place in this world at this moment for any but the mother's tears. The rest are obscene. I curse them all. Because I am in pain. I wish everyone would go away. As far away from me as possible. I wish the priests would stop mouthing gentle platitudes and instead speak the truth and talk about the anger in the hearts of mothers who have lost a child, of the fury in their bellies when they see the blank face that once suckled at their breast. I am bent double on this slab of marble and I am mad with rage. Cursed be this stone that I did not choose and that now covers my child for eternity. I look around and I spit on the ground. I will never come here again. I will not lay any wreaths. I will not water any of the flowers and will never pray. There will not be any contemplation. I will not speak to this stone, with my head lowered and the defeated demeanour of a war widow. I will never come here again because there is nothing here. Pippo is not here. I curse everyone who wept around me, believing that was what had to be done on such an occasion. I know, and I repeat, Pippo is not here.'

V
I Grant You Vengeance
(September 1980)

Matteo's journeys continued, always from one point in the city to another, late at night when cats were greedily tearing open the waste bags put out behind restaurants by men eager to finish their working day. He worked less and less. How many times had he seen a customer raise their arm at the sight of his taxi and passed by without stopping? He just couldn't do it. He was too far away, too deep in thought. He drove so that he did not have to think of anything practical. And so the nights followed on one from the other.

But, one evening, Giuliana caught him by the sleeve. Everything had been calm. He had heated up some supper before he left, as usual. She had come in at the moment he was clearing away his plate. She had not said anything. Neither had he. He had risen somewhat wearily; she had gone to fetch the documents for the car and the keys, and as he opened the door, he felt her grasp his arm with astonishing force. She faced him, her countenance transformed. Her lips were trembling as if her mouth was reluctant to say the words burning inside her. He was stupefied. Where had this anger suddenly come from? What had provoked this crisis? She was still not letting go of his arm. He hesitated. He realised he was unsure what force was driving his wife. Was it anger? Or was it distress? Did she want to fight with him, yell at him, hit him or simply hold him back for a few minutes so that she could cry in his arms? He didn't know.

But, finally, Giuliana did speak, in that voice, broken with grief, and he understood that it was anger that rose to her lips. He also understood that her anger must have accumulated over weeks and that her habitual silence, which he had been too quick to assume was resignation to her fate, had in fact been the long preparation for this moment.

'What are you doing, Matteo?' she demanded. And since he did not reply, she repeated aggressively, 'What are you doing?'

'I'm going out,' he said simply. And he added, in order to demonstrate that this was usual, just what happened on any normal day, 'It's time.'

Then her anger burst out and she began to shout, like a fury, 'To do what, Matteo? To trail from one place to another? To wait for daybreak so that you can come back and hide here? What are you doing, Matteo?'

He stood open-mouthed, amazed that she knew what he did when he went out, that she knew perfectly well what state he wandered about in, although he had never spoken of it. It was as if he found himself naked in front of her. He felt ashamed. He was about to say that he would not talk about it with her, but she did not give him a chance. She began to strike him on the chest. The blows to his torso, accompanied by sounds that were a blend of groans and curses, were not intended to bruise him but rather to shake something free in him, something that remained stubbornly stuck. He let her do it, thinking that it would calm her, but then she said, even more angrily, the words accompanied by tears that shook him more than her clenched fists, which continued to pummel him: 'Bring me my son, Matteo. Bring him back to me, and if you can't, at least give me the one who killed him!'

He almost lost his balance. His mind whirled with Giuliana's words, Pippo's face, the scene of the shoot-out, his useless wanderings. He could neither speak nor stay a moment longer with Giuliana. He pushed her hands gently away and she let him, with the docility of a child. He opened the front door and, without a word, left the apartment and ran down the stairs.

As he made for his car, he was afraid he would fall over. His legs were trembling. He knew he was pale. There was a buzzing in his ears that grew louder. It was only once he was sitting in his car, and clutching the steering wheel firmly, that he regained his composure. He started the car and began to drive aimlessly. As Naples unfurled before his eyes, he thought about Giuliana: he saw her face contorted with anger, grimacing through her tears. She was beautiful and so much stronger than he was. She was more far-sighted than he was and was able to look their tragedy in the eye. She had just asked him something and she was right to do so. If he brought Giuliana the head of the murderer, it would not bring their son back to them, but perhaps they would be able to start living again. For the first time since Pippo's death, he felt a warm strength coursing through his veins. Now he was heading for the port and he drove at breakneck speed. He was filled with new ardour. He felt strong, and determined on a course that nothing could deflect him from. He was going to be patient but brutal, clever but brave and he would find his son's murderer. And then his wife with her beautiful grieving face would be able to smile again.

A few days later, Matteo went into a café on Via Roma and looked round at the customers in there. A man of about forty raised his hand and waved Matteo over. It was the police officer in charge of solving Pippo's murder. Three days earlier, Matteo had rung the number he had been given by the police at the time of the investigation and a weary-sounding voice had proposed this meeting.

Matteo would never have recognised him. Yet he had met him, had been interviewed by him, but it had been just after Pippo's murder, when nothing mattered, and no face or word or experience made any impression on him.

The inspector ordered a second cup of coffee. He looked tired and Matteo wondered if that was his normal manner. Or maybe he had been dreading this meeting and was keen to get the painful task of telling a father that no one would ever know who had murdered his son over with as soon as possible.

Matteo asked calmly but forcefully whether the investigation had made any progress. The inspector looked at him for a long time before replying. He was trying to assess from Matteo's demeanour whether he should employ the usual soothing but misleading platitudes, and tell him, for example, that everything was proceeding normally, that it would take time, of course, but that eventually they would catch the killers, or whether he should speak frankly. He chose the second option, either because he was too tired that day to lie, or because he had seen a determination in Matteo's eye that encouraged him to be honest.

'There's no progress, Signor De Nittis,' he said. 'There never is in these cases.'

Matteo said nothing and the inspector knew he had made the right choice, that the man before him was ready to hear what he was going to tell him and that it would actually be a greater comfort to him than all the meaningless phrases he could summon.

'Tell me everything you know about the case,' said Matteo. He wanted the inspector to see how firmly he had made up his mind, and how he would not be frightened off by the risks he might face. The police officer gave a little sigh, full of sympathy for this father who sought, in the details of the investigation, some scraps of comfort to relieve the grief that nothing could make better, and willingly complied.

Two factions were engaged in a fierce battle for control of the city. On one side was the Forcella faction; on the other, the Secondigliano clan. The latter, younger and more violent, wanted to lay their hands on the traditional strongholds of the Camorra. In the weeks preceding Pippo's death, there had already been numerous crimes and acts of violence. It was most likely, according to the inspector – but this was a personal theory, nothing more – that the man who'd fired the first shot was from Forcella. Because, that same day, men from Forcella had stormed into a bar in Secondigliano and killed two men. So it looked very much as if the Forcella clan was fighting back. In addition, and this was more significant, they had found a body near the port, ten days after the shoot-out, wounded in the shoulder, his head blown apart by a bullet to the mouth. That man was from the Secondigliano clan. And he was no doubt the man who had been the target of the shooting in Vicolo della Pace. Despite his shoulder injury he had managed to escape into the maze of little streets. However, this was not his home turf and the killers had found him a few hours later and finished him off triumphantly. This was all supposition, of course, and since no witnesses had come forward it was impossible to get any evidence, but it was what the inspector believed had happened.

'Give me a name,' said Matteo. He was burning with a new excitement. All through the inspector's account, his foot had been tapping under the table.

The inspector did not reply. He slowly looked up at Matteo and asked, 'What is it that you want, Signor De Nittis?'

Matteo hesitated. It was his turn to weigh up what he could say to this man and what it would be wiser to keep quiet about. Would he understand? Matteo thought he would, so he replied, his eyes shining with rage, 'What I want is to find the man who did this. And to make him pay.'

'Why?' asked the inspector, and Matteo understood that he had done the right thing in speaking frankly. The policeman had not been appalled; he had probably been aware of Matteo's desire for vengeance since the beginning of the meeting, and that had probably made the encounter more bearable. It would have been far worse had Matteo sobbed and groaned and clutched his jacket. At least this way, they were talking man to man. Nevertheless, the inspector went on, not unsympathetically, 'So that I will be obliged to arrest you, and you will end up in jail, surrounded by the very men who have ruined your life? You're better than that, Signor De Nittis.'

'No', said Matteo urgently. 'Because my wife asked me to.'

The inspector was silent at that. He had to admit that was

not what he had expected. He lowered his eyes, so that Matteo would not see how disturbed he was. Then he rose, smiled slightly and left without saying another word.

'What's wrong?' Matteo had just returned home and found Giuliana standing in the kitchen crying. As he asked the question, he realised how nonsensical it was. He knew exactly what was wrong and why she was crying. A few minutes earlier, she had been calmly preparing the evening meal. She had laid the table. The water for the pasta had begun to simmer. And, suddenly, it was as if she had been struck. And then nothing had existed for her except her grief. That was how it was. Since Pippo's death, despair stalked them constantly, surprising them at moments they least expected it. He was well aware of the sadness that had overwhelmed his wife.

'What's wrong?' he could not help asking again, to rouse her from her misery. She looked at him and smiled sadly. In that moment, she felt she had found her husband again. The gentle way he had posed the question, the worry in his eyes as he repeated it, were things she had not encountered in him for a long time. They had already become so distant from each other that his kindness in asking and repeating the question – the mixture of worried eagerness and gentle solicitude – overwhelmed her. She smiled through her tears. 'I can't go on,' she said simply.

Matteo sat down and took her hand. He didn't say anything and she was grateful for that because just then there were no words that could comfort her and it would have been torture had he spoken. His silence was like a balm. Cautiously, she hugged him.

'I want you to bring him back to me, Matteo,' she said, her voice sounding strange, thin but at the same time decided. 'Why aren't you going to fetch him?'

This time her voice broke into a sob. And still he said nothing, and she was thankful that he did not mock her, did not tell her that it was not possible, but simply held her more tightly in his arms. She had just revealed to her husband what she felt deep inside, the mad longing to go and get her son from where he was, so that she could hold him close and breathe in his smell, just one more time. 'They've killed us, Matteo,' she added. 'Death is here. Within us. It contaminates everything. It is so far inside us that it will never come out.'

'I will get him,' replied Matteo with a new determination in his voice. The idea of vengeance had returned. He wasn't sure if that would appease her but he was certain that it would at least bring them closer. That was all they had, an all-consuming hatred. 'I swear, Giuliana. I will get him,' and they closed their eyes so that they could focus on the bitter joy they hoped would come.

A little while later, Matteo received a letter. When he discovered it in the letter box, he knew straight away that there was something out of the ordinary about it and, as he climbed the stairs, he carried it with a sort of impatience and apprehension.

He waited until he was sitting at the kitchen table before opening it. Inside the envelope there was nothing but a photo. There was no card or scrap of paper clipped to it, no signature, just an old photo with worn corners, a little torn on one side, an old black and white photo of a man, full length, looking straight at the camera with a cheeky, easy-going smile. The face had been circled in pen, and a name added: 'Toto Cullaccio' along with an address: '7 Vicolo Giganti'.

Matteo sat there for a long time, holding the photo. He smiled. He no longer wondered who had sent him the picture. It could have been anyone, the policeman he had met, overtaken by sudden remorse, a neighbour, a stranger, anyone. He did not even think of that any more. He looked at the photo and it was obvious that he was looking at his son's murderer. He did not need the sender to have included a note; he understood. Toto Cullaccio. So that was who had done it. All he had to do now was find him, and slit his stomach open.

When he headed out of the apartment, he left the photo on the kitchen table. He had decided to go out for the day. He wanted Giuliana to find it there, in the silence of the apartment, so that she would have the time and leisure to meditate on her desire for vengeance.

He walked in the direction of the market in Forcella. He had the killer's name and that made him smile. When he plunged into the crowds in the little streets, he felt Naples shout and sweat around him. In the market, the crowd was already dense and there were numerous stalls set up on the pavement. Neapolitans were selling fish, fruit and vegetables, chinaware and clothes. Further on, Asians were selling toys and shoes – sandals of all types and colours – and still further away, Africans were pushing large tables on wheels covered in swimsuits and T-shirts. Here and there on the ground, unlicensed vendors displayed collections of fake handbags and sunglasses. The poorest vendors, perhaps Pakistani, had laid out posters and pictures of kittens or dolphins, photos of American stars or Italian footballers. You could find everything here. People who lived here came to buy their food or clothes, or to wander about, pay off their debts, or do deals. Matteo walked in amongst the confusion of trestle tables, thinking all the time of that man, who was certainly here somewhere in these streets. Perhaps they had just passed each other. Perhaps they could both hear the same trader shouting how fresh his meat was. Toto Cullaccio. Matteo was drunk on the name. Toto Cullaccio. He could have shouted the name at the top of his voice. Instead he greedily repeated it in his head.

That evening, when he entered the apartment, Giuliana was in the kitchen. He went in to join her. The photo was still there, on view. She had seen it, she had picked it up and studied it with feelings of rage. She had understood that this was the man, then she had put it back on the table, waiting for Matteo to return so that they could share the victory.

He was on the point of asking her whether she had looked at the picture, but she spoke first and said in a voice that almost made him jump: 'I never want to hear that name said in this house.'

She looked deeply into his eyes, standing straight and tall like a soldier facing danger.

'I'm going this evening,' he said.

She regarded him intently, as if to verify that he was really saying what she thought he had said. She did not ask him to repeat it. She had read in his eyes the confirmation she sought.

'When you come home, I will wash his blood from your shirt,' she replied simply.

He looked at her without saying anything, then he went to the wardrobe and took out the old pistol his uncle had left him, loaded it and put it in his pocket. She watched him calmly, with gratitude. Revenge was, for the moment, the only form their love could take. She thanked him for his courage, for agreeing to be, for a few moments, a killer in the streets, the hand that held a weapon and did not flinch. She thanked him for the murder he was going to commit, because it told her he believed in her, Giuliana, and that he was prepared to share the burden of her anger.

VI
The Kiss of Grace
(August 2002)

I head back into the bowels of the city. I'm not afraid any more. Naples is here, at my feet, and she will keep me hidden. I can take my time. Toto Cullaccio must still be screaming in the cemetery. I imagine I can hear him. I picture him waving his stumps at the sky, blood running down his sleeves, scaring the cats, rats and clouds away. My sweet, bloody victory. My horror, my disfigurement. I'm happy. I took two fingers with me. I didn't plan to, but I needed proof of my success. One finger for Grace, another for my father.

I drive slowly in the evening air, leaving Cullaccio to writhe like a three-legged beast who can no longer walk. He looks like the figures I see at night. I've spent so many nights fighting off the wild creatures which claw at my mind, trying to devour me. He has the same awful face as those spirits. For twenty years, those faces have haunted my sleep. I didn't shudder when I saw Cullaccio's face contorted in pain, because I'm used to it. I've seen souls more tormented than that. I come from a place where Cullaccio's cries wouldn't even be heard. There was so much groaning and wailing there, so much ugliness and fear, the thought of it still makes me shudder.

Naples seems quiet. A beautiful, sleeping city, rocking gently like the boats in the harbour. There's nothing to be afraid of now. I feel calm. The police won't catch me and nor will Cullaccio's men. I'll disappear into the backstreets like a cat slinking along the side of the road. I'm glad I didn't kill Cullaccio. He'll go to hell helpless, treading uncertainly, shaking like an old man, the wounds on his hands barely healed. He'll sink into those depths bearing the mark of my vengeance, and that way everyone will see that he belongs to me, that I've made him my monster.

The car keeps moving along the avenues, heading down towards the port. I breathe calmly. I want to see Grace one last time before I go. I can't go to the café to hug my father – the father who's still alive –without putting him in danger. But I can go and see Grace. I know where to find her. The roads of Naples gradually open up to me, like trees in an enchanted forest parting to let me through.

There she is, right in front of me. It wasn't hard to find her – she's in Piazza Carmine, where she always is. I look at her tenderly. Grace, my tired, loving aunt. Grace, my shy, haggard mother. Her lips are starting to droop. She wears so much make-up. For twenty years she's worked the streets. For twenty years, she's borne the weight of Naples, heard its muffled cries. They've called her names, mocked her broad shoulders, her deep voice, her heavy stride and large hands, but they've kept her close, even paid her for sex, however revolting they claim to find her. Grace has smiled through it, the same sad smile for the past two decades. Although they'd never admit it, she's been there for them, and they love her for it. She knows them and never gives up on them, even now. For how much longer will you be the black Virgin of the port, Grace? Will you ever be seen shuffling along the streets like a little old lady? The years go by but you keep coming back, made up like a faded diva. Grace.

I stand facing her and she waves me into a corner so that we can talk. She kisses me the way you kiss a child. I'm the son who'll never take after her. The son she never had.

'What's up?' she asks.

I tell her calmly that I'm leaving. She seems surprised, but doesn't ask questions.

'I've started,' I say.

'Started what?' she asks, mildly curious, as if I were telling her about a school project.

'Getting my revenge,' I say, as I take one of Cullaccio's fingers out of my pocket. Look, Grace. I show her. It's the finger he shot with. For twenty years he's got off scot-free. Not any more. He's squirming in pain, howling like a dog.

'What have you done?' she asks, her face suddenly seized by fear.

'I'm leaving.'

I drop the finger on the ground. I didn't bring it for her to hold on to. It's not a keepsake. I just wanted her to see it. I've dropped it on the pavement like a scrap of paper or a piece of rubbish. If Toto Cullaccio is scattered around in bits, his body parts feeding the pigeons and rats, that's fine by me.

'Where are you going?' Grace asks, clutching my hand.

I look at her, surprised. I thought she'd have guessed.

'To look for my father,' I say.

She stares hard at me and then says something which catches me off guard.

'You won't find him. Things like that don't happen more than once.'

I know she won't stop me leaving. She won't try to stand in the way of what I want, but I'm surprised she's against the idea. I thought she'd be pleased I've finally worked up the courage to make the journey. It's taken me twenty years, after all. There's nothing left to say. I plant a gentle kiss on her cheek and hope she understands that this is my way of telling her that I love her. Grace. Mistress of the port. Wife to every scumbag and joker who spends his summer nights pissing away his pathetic life.

'He's not the only one who's been in hell for the past twenty years.'

She says this as our cheeks touch. Her smooth voice gets

inside my head. I step back, confused. 'Who?' I ask.

'Your mother,' she replies without a smile, without any expression, only an aura of calm. I look at her and she looks straight back at me, holding my gaze. She waits for me to say something. I smile.

'You're the only mother I have,' I say as I turn to leave.

VII
Garibaldo's Café
(September 1980)

'Now I won't be able to go home,' thought Matteo, forlornly retracing his steps.

He felt exhausted, empty. 'I'm a coward,' he murmured, looking at the ground, 'a coward, and nothing can save me.' A few minutes earlier he had aimed his weapon at the man's face. A few minutes earlier, time had stood still and then, without him knowing why, he had lowered his arm and the man had fled, disappearing round the corner with the speed of a cat bolting at the sound of a firecracker.

He would have liked to sit down on a bench or on the steps of a church so that time would go by, so that he could wait, doing nothing until his strength returned, so that he could forgive himself, so that his humiliating feeling of shame would pass, but it began to rain and he had to find somewhere to shelter. 'I'll drive until I don't have a drop of petrol left,' he thought and hurried back to where he had left his car.

That night he drove all over Naples, randomly taking whichever routes presented themselves, without trying to work out where he was, or where the road he was on led, finding he was suddenly at a monument or square that he knew well but that he had not expected to loom up at that moment, thinking he was elsewhere in the city. He drove and the city was nothing but a succession of red lights, then green lights, then red ones again.

At one point that night, without especially meaning to, he ended up at the port. He liked it here. The streets here had the same air of silent sadness that he felt. There were no people, no shops. He lowered the window to breathe the salty air from the far-off sea. The engine ticked over as he waited for the light to turn green. He turned it off. There were no cars in sight and he wanted to hear the noises of the night around him.

That was when a woman appeared. He had not seen her coming. She had emerged from nowhere and she was breathless. She leant against the window. For a brief moment he thought she was going to proposition him – she wore eye make-up and lipstick. In spite of the fact that the night was warm, she wore a heavy red coat with a fake-fur collar. He raised his hand in a gesture of refusal but she didn't give him time to speak.

She said, in a voice he found unnaturally deep: 'Santa Maria del Purgatorio Church, please … On Spaccanapoli.'

He was about to say that he wasn't working, that she was going to have to find another taxi, because, that night, he wasn't interested in taking customers, didn't care if people were in a hurry to get somewhere, didn't care either about churches or what was going on, but again she was too quick for him.

She said, with a sort of nervous urgency in her voice: 'Hurry, I have to get to confession.'

That left him speechless. It must have been four in the morning. Here the two of them were in a district that was as ugly as a dead dog on the side of the road and she was talking about church and confession like a little boy in a hurry to do a wee, as if she could barely contain the words that threatened to spill out at any moment.

He sat there stupefied by the woman's sudden appearance, and she opened the back door and climbed into the car. Then, rather than fight to force her to get out, rather than have to talk to explain that he would not be taking her anywhere because that night he was anything but a taxi driver, rather than do any of that, he settled himself in his seat and set off.

As they bowled along in silence, from time to time Matteo glanced in the rear-view mirror. There was something strange about her, but, not being able to put his finger on what it was, he circled it like a cat around food that has an unfamiliar smell.

She had opened her bag and was redoing her make-up. Looking at her more carefully, Matteo could immediately see that she was trying to get rid of traces of blood that she had at the corner of her mouth and to cover a bruise on her forehead with powder. He did not ask her about it. He wasn't interested. He was not in danger, he felt no threat and that was all that counted. He couldn't have cared less if she had been involved in a fight.

When he arrived in front of the church and turned the ignition off, she leant forward and started talking in a solicitous voice. Again he was surprised by her voice. He felt her breath on his shoulder and he understood, from the way she was speaking, that she was trying to be ingratiating and friendly.

'I have a little problem,' she said.

He looked up at her in the rear-view mirror but said nothing.

She gave an embarrassed smile. 'I don't have any money on me.'

He did not reply. He was annoyed by it all. It was all beside the point. He was not the slightest bit concerned about the sum of money she owed him, but she took his silence for anger and hastened to add, 'Here's what I suggest. I go in and confess—'

'At this hour?' interrupted Matteo.

'Yes, yes, don't worry, it's all arranged … So, I'll go into the church and you can go and have a drink opposite. When I've finished, I'll pay for whatever you've had.'

Matteo turned his head. Opposite the church, there was a kind of pedestrianised arcade. There were a few shops, a greengrocer, a tailor. And he was surprised to see there was also a little bar and that, in spite of the lateness of the hour, there were lights on inside.

'There?' he asked.

'Yes, I know the owner. He'll put everything on my tab. Is that all right?'

Matteo did not answer, but he did put the handbrake on. He did not know why he was going along with it. It was not for the sake of the money she owed him. Perhaps it was just to pass the time, and because he was desperate for a drink and did not have the energy to go home.

They both got out of the car. He watched her go up the steps of the church and knock on the heavy bronze door. A very long time passed. He smiled. This was all ridiculous. No one went to confession at this hour of night. He was about to return to his car and leave her to her lie, demonstrating that he did not want her money, when suddenly, to his great surprise, the door opened a little and the woman disappeared with a faint tapping of sharp heels on marble. So rather than go back to his car, rather than go driving round the city for hours, he decided to stick to what they had agreed and pushed the door to the café, which opened with a dragging sound like an old dog yawning.

The café was empty. Or almost. As Matteo entered, he saw only one customer, sitting at a table at the back. He was a well-built bald man in his fifties whose features Matteo could not make out because he was bent over a pile of papers that he was studying with great concentration. His table was covered in sheets of paper, files, pens and newspaper cuttings. At the bar, a tall man was slowly wiping half-clean glasses. He looked tired.

'What can I get you?' asked the owner.

'A glass of white wine,' replied Matteo, wondering why the man had kept the café open. It was four in the morning. There was only one customer, two now, which wasn't nearly enough to justify keeping the place open. 'Strange world,' Matteo said to himself, thinking no more about the reasons for the late opening. He drank his wine. Then he ordered a second glass. He drank so as not to think about anything, and the others in the café did not break the silence that had settled over them so completely that he felt as if you could actually see it floating in the air like layers of dust.

He jumped when, almost an hour later, the door opened. The woman he had dropped off by the church in the square had just walked in. He had totally forgotten about her and was surprised by the warmth with which she came directly over to him. 'There you are!'

She nodded a greeting to the owner and boomed at him,

'Garibaldo, everything this gentleman has drunk and will drink tonight is on me.'

Then she went up to Matteo and held out her hand. 'I didn't even introduce myself: Graziella. But I prefer to be called Grace, American-style; it's more chic.'

And she laughed uproariously as she shook Matteo's hand. That was when he understood. What had intrigued him in the car, what he hadn't been able to identify or name, was now obvious. 'She's a man!' he thought. That explained her deep voice, her coarse features, her stature and her excessive use of feminine gestures.

'Matteo,' he replied curtly then looked down. He didn't wish to be rude, but he hoped she would go and get a drink for herself, leaving him to his silence.

'Don Mazerotti is a saint,' she said and Matteo understood that he would not be left in peace, and that, short of getting up and leaving, he was going to have to talk to her.

'If he heard your confession in the middle of the night, he must be!' he murmured without really believing what he was saying.

'Exactly!' agreed Graziella, taking a comb from her bag and rearranging her hair. 'He's the only one, you know, the only one in the whole of Naples, who welcomes us.'

Matteo didn't know what she meant by 'us' but he preferred not to ask.

'If you knew how many churches have thrown me out as if I were depraved ... He never does that. Never. Even though it causes him problems. They want to hound him out of his church. That's why he locks himself in. But we're here for him; we won't let that happen, will we, Garibaldo?'

She nodded conspiratorially at the owner, who replied, half

amused, half weary, 'True enough, Grace. We won't let a man like Don Mazerotti down.'

Then she went on talking, talking a lot about many different things, frequently seeking the opinion of the owner, drinking what he served her and indicating that she wanted a refill each time her glass was empty. She spoke of the city, which was getting more and more ugly, and of the encounters you had at night that left you with the urgent desire to go to confession. She talked and talked and Matteo drank along with her. When she saw that Matteo was succumbing to fatigue and that his head was nodding forward onto the table, she took matters into her own hands and told him, 'You need a cup of coffee, a real one. The kind that acts as a pick-me-up. Do you know that Garibaldo has a gift for making coffee for all occasions?'

He looked at her uncomprehendingly. So she explained what she meant: 'Garibaldo can make the coffee suit the occasion. No one knows what he puts in it, what ingredients he uses, but he knows exactly how to make coffee to suit the precise needs of the customer. He goes into the back of the café to make these coffees. He has a special percolator there, probably surrounded by a multitude of little boxes of spices and all sorts of ingredients: pepper, cumin, orange blossom, grappa, lemon, wine, vinegar, chilli powder ... He prepares his mixture there and it never takes more time than preparing a normal coffee. And no customer has ever complained. The desired effect is always achieved: coffee to keep you awake without sleep for three nights in a row or to give you the strength of two men, relaxing coffee, aphrodisiac coffee ... He only has one rule: the person who requests the coffee must be the one to drink it. Garibaldo does not wish to poison anyone.' Grace finished her story by saying triumphantly,

'This is where I will come to drink my last coffee when I feel death is coming …'

'It will not come. It is already here …'

All three jumped at the sound of the voice. It came from the man sitting at the table at the back, who had looked up from his papers. His intervention was greeted by embarrassed silence.

'I'm sorry?' asked Grace, a bit put out, and, turning back to Garibaldo and Matteo, she murmured, 'I think we've woken old Provolone!'

The two men tried not to smile, because it was true that with his big bald head and no neck the man did actually resemble those cheeses in the shape of a thick sausage that were sold in grocers' shops all over the city.

But the stranger continued, 'Don't you feel it here? Death? It's all around us, surrounding us, and no one can escape it.'

'Are you an expert?' asked Matteo in the irritated tone of someone forced to talk when they want to be alone.

'Yes, in a way, I am,' replied the man, adjusting his jacket. 'I'm a follower of Pietro Bartolomeo.'

'Who?' demanded Garibaldo.

'Archbishop Bartolomeo of Antioch,' replied the man. 'He died in 1311 in Palermo.'

'And he talks to you at night?' asked Grace mischievously.

'No,' the man replied calmly. 'He's buried in the crypt of Palermo Cathedral. There's a beautiful catafalque. Astounding. It's there that I had the revelation at the age of thirty-five. I was contemplating the tomb, laid out amongst dozens of others, all like boxes of useless marble, and my gaze was attracted to the sculpture adorning it. At each corner of the catafalque, faces had been engraved, and on the side of

71

the tomb, a double door. Each side of the door was decorated with two ram's heads. But what was astonishing was that the door engraved on the tomb was slightly open. I was stupefied. It was as if the dead man was telling us that the gate to the afterlife was ajar. I was then in a hurry to read the writings of Bartolomeo of Antioch and, when I did, my eyes were opened: the two worlds are permeable. What a revelation! Ever since, I have been studying that idea. I have analysed texts. From Orpheus to Theseus. From Alexander the Great to Ulysses. Believe me, I have searched in the furthest corners of the libraries in Palermo and Bari, finding books that have not been opened for centuries. This is true. I have looked everywhere. Nothing has escaped me. I have been all over Italy, in Naples, Palermo, Lecce, Matera. I have written hundreds of pages. But no one has read them. I am regarded as a madman. Everywhere I have been, I have received the same embarrassed, slightly mocking looks. The Dean of Lecce University actually summoned me to his office, to tell me that my work was an insult to scientific thought, would you believe, and that it would ruin my career ambitions in all the universities in the region. I was considered a fantasist. And this was long before I was discovered in the gardens by the port, my trousers round my knees, if you will excuse the expression, with a delicious boy of fifteen. But it makes no difference. I persevered. I know what I've read. I haven't made anything up.'

'And so what?' interrupted Matteo impatiently.

The professor took his time before replying. He did not want to let himself be rushed by Matteo's ill temper.

'Do you know,' he said, 'that Frederick II declared war on death? ... No? ... That doesn't surprise me. No one knows that. But it's true. He descended into the Underworld with his army. He went in through the Càlena Abbey passage, in Gargano, one night in summer 1221, with thirty thousand men. The descent took five hours. I know that. I read it. Five long hours during which soldiers disappeared behind the thick walls surrounding the abbey and did not reappear. He had given battle. Fiercely. He wanted to kill death. That is why, much later, he built the Castel del Monte, an octagonal building that dominates the countryside and the sea. Castel del Monte, his tomb for eternity. He wanted to ensure he could not be taken. And death did not find him. It was never able to consume him. It is said that he can still be seen, on certain summer nights, diving into the water, in the middle of Peschici Bay or off the coast of Trani, with all his warriors ready at his side. He's continuing his war.'

Everyone had been listening with a kind of childlike wonderment.

'I've never heard of such a thing,' murmured Grace.

'That's why he was excommunicated,' the professor went on. 'In 1245. Pope Innocent IV did not want him associated with Christianity and wished to make him appear possessed.'

'And you?' asked Matteo. 'You know things no one else knows?'

He had asked the question with the eagerness of a child, avid to learn something that would relieve his pain.

'I know that death eats at our hearts,' replied the professor, looking Matteo straight in the eye. 'This is true. I know that death lives in us and grows and grows throughout our lives.'

Matteo felt as if the professor was speaking about him. He shook his head like a tired horse. 'You're right,' he said. Everything was coming back to him. Tiredness. The weight of mourning. He wanted to get rid of all that, if only for a moment, like removing a heavy cloak of suffering and putting it on the ground. And then, without really knowing why, he began to speak. Without stopping. Without looking up. The three men in the café were silent and no one interrupted him. He spoke in order to empty himself of the lava that was burning his soul.

'I should have killed a man today. Toto Cullaccio. I had him in my sights. He was right there looking down the barrel of my gun, and I lowered my arm. I don't know why. He is the man who murdered my son. A little boy of six, dead in my arms before I could say a word to him. When I think of my son, of his life cut short, when I think of mine stretching uselessly into eternity, I do not understand what it is all about. The world is small and I will be like a prisoner tearing my flesh against its walls. So he did well, your Frederick II. And too bad that he was excommunicated. That means nothing! There is nothing to fear anywhere. The heavens. The Pope. Nothing. You know why? Because the heavens are empty and everything is upside down. I had hoped for punishment for the murderers and paradise for the innocents. I really did. I hoped for that. With all my soul. But men wreck everything and they have nothing to fear. That's how the world is. And you know what is left for us?'

He turned towards Garibaldo and Graziella, as if appealing for everyone's opinion, but, as no one replied, he went on, 'Only one thing is left for us. Either courage or cowardice. Nothing else.'

Then without waiting for a response and with the haste of someone who regrets having given himself away, he nodded at the little group and left.

VIII
Giuliana's Night
(September 1980)

When he got home and pushed the door open, Matteo knew at once that Giuliana was waiting for him, despite the lateness of the hour. He went into the flat. She was there, as he had imagined her, sitting at the living-room table. For Giuliana, time had crawled by horribly slowly. She had wondered what was happening. She had tried to imagine the scene of the murder, the moment that Matteo had fired. Then she had begun to worry. He was still not home. Perhaps something had happened to him? There was nothing she could do but wait. If only day would break. If only her husband would return or something would happen. If only the telephone would ring or the police would knock on the door. In the end, she resigned herself to the wait, sitting at the table, promising herself she would not move until something happened.

When she heard the key in the lock, she smiled, but did not move. She was desperate to see him, so that he would tell her everything, and she would hug him and bandage his wounds, filled with happiness at revenge exacted. But when she saw him, the colour drained from her face. He was in front of her and his shirt had no bloodstains on it. And she could see straight away from his embarrassed demeanour that nothing had happened, but she could not help asking, 'What happened?'

'Nothing,' replied Matteo, lowering his eyes. There was an

awkward silence. He knew what she was thinking. That it was not an answer. That it was not what she expected from him. That she would want nothing more to do with a man whose courage extended only as far as disappearing for hours and then returning tired and sheepish. Her pent-up rage would not be satisfied by that.

Her jaw stiffened. The longer the silence stretched the more cowardly Matteo felt. Then, just to say something, so that she would look at him with something other than reproach, he asked her in a childish voice, 'Did you know that Frederick II was excommunicated?'

She said nothing, her lips parted. Her eyes expressed neither anger nor consternation. She was simply thinking how her husband was now a stranger to her and how infinitely far apart they had grown. She said, 'No,' almost in spite of herself. No. She did not know that. She had never even thought that there would come a day when they would discuss it. And she probably did not want to know anything about Frederick II and the Pope, because all that concerned her, on that nauseous night of sadness, was whether she would one day have the head of the man who had torn her son from her, whether her husband would have the strength one night to come home a little paler than usual, still out of breath from his long run in the streets of their district, with the blood of the murderer on his shirt. There was no room for anything else in her. And he understood that the instant she said 'No'. He knew that he would not be able to describe the strange hours he had spent in the café in the company of those three men with whom he had shared a moment of his life that he did not understand. He would not be able to explain how that time, now that he thought about it, had been perhaps a kind of happiness, or, at least, the respite he had vainly been seeking during those months of defeat and grief. He had felt good, at peace and able to forget himself. He would have loved to describe this to Giuliana, but he did not. She would have laughed. Or struck him.

Giuliana stood up suddenly. She came and went from one room to another, showing no haste or emotion, just a resigned determination, which gave every movement she made an air of finality.

'Giuliana,' he said, softly, because her coldness was frightening to him.

She stopped between two bedrooms and said to him, 'I would have washed your shirt. I wanted the water in the bath to turn red with blood so that I could soak my hands in it. But you did nothing, Matteo. You came back here and you brought nothing with you.'

He knew that there was nothing he could say. He had promised to kill the man and had not done it. But he didn't want her to look at him like that, with that air of repulsed disgust.

'Giuliana,' he repeated. He wanted to tell her she could rely on him, that everything could still go on, that he would find a way. She did not let him look at her with tenderness.

She said in a hard voice, 'It will always be between us, Matteo. Until the end of our lives. What you did not do.'

Then, without hesitating, she went into the bedroom and pulled a suitcase onto the bed – the same one they had used ten years earlier for their honeymoon in Sorrento. Matteo watched her sadly. She took some underwear, a few pieces of jewellery, some things from the kitchen and from Pippo's bedroom, but he didn't know which things, because he did not have the strength to follow her there. It took her no more than twenty minutes to assemble her life's possessions.

She was leaving. Because, from the moment he had pushed open the door with that expression of resigned fatigue, she had seen, with absolute certainty, that there was nothing more for her in the flat, or in their relationship that she could lean on. She wasn't annoyed with Matteo. What could he do? It was time to leave and that was that. There was nothing to be said. It would make no sense to reproach him. They couldn't do anything for each other any more, except wound each other by being together, with their painful memories and their secret tears.

In just half an hour she was ready – suitcase in hand, a raincoat over her shoulders. He had not moved. He wasn't sure he wanted to stop her. For him also, deep down, her departure seemed the natural conclusion to this long day. The logical outcome of those long months of grief they had endured like silent and obedient workhorses.

They looked at each other in silence. Talking seemed pointless. What could they say? Neither of them was at fault. Neither of them had taken the decision to part like this. It was simply down to their misfortunes. Life had dealt them a terrible blow and there was no way now for them to recover.

She raised her hand in a small gesture – as if to caress his cheek – signifying that she did not blame him for anything and that at that moment of her departure she wanted to recall the tenderness they had shared – but she could not complete the movement and her hand stayed suspended in mid-air, before falling with the slowness of the defeated back to her side. He must have understood her last attempt to reach out, because he had a strange smile on his lips – more of gratitude than joy – then he let her pass.

'She's leaving,' he thought. Giuliana, his beloved wife; Giuliana, the mother of his son, her love destroyed; Giuliana, more courageous than he, because she was doing what had to be done whilst he had not had the strength. Giuliana, whom life had abused, who should have smiled for thirty more years, then withered gently away, without violence, like a little apple still beautiful with the patina life bestows when it has been kind. Giuliana had become ugly, so suddenly, with empty eyes and drawn features. Giuliana who was turning her back on her life without a moment's hesitation. 'She's leaving.' He smelt her perfume for the last time and let her pass. Giuliana had just left him, with the unfinished gesture of a woman who regretted not being able to love any more.

Outside the front door of the building, she crossed the road and walked over to the opposite pavement, put her case down and took her time looking up at the façade of the place she had lived for so long. Matteo was up there. The light was on. He must be walking about in the apartment. Or else he had sunk into an armchair. Had he come to the window they could have seen each other one last time, but he did not. Giuliana thought about him. Focusing totally on him. She tried to revive memories that might help her remember him with love, but she kept coming up against what he had failed to do. She kept coming up against his cowardice. So with a look of disgust on her face, she uttered a second curse, which was only heard by the starving cats in the area:

'I curse you, Matteo. Like the others. Because you're as worthless as they are. It is a cowardly world that lets children die and fathers tremble. I curse you because you did not shoot. What made you hesitate? An unexpected noise? The shadow of someone passing in the distance? Cullaccio's pleading expression? You must have been distracted when what was needed was to be deaf to everything around you. Bullets don't have thoughts, Matteo. You had agreed to be my bullet. I curse you because for all those years you stood at my side, discreet and loyal – but you could not prevent catastrophe and could not put it right. What use are you, Matteo? I counted on your strength. On the day of the funeral you held me tight so that I would not collapse. You always thought there was a sort of glory in enduring moments of pain with stoicism and restraint. I didn't, Matteo. I didn't care about that. It would have been better if my legs had given way and I had emptied all the water from my body, by crying, spitting and snivelling like a beast. You stopped me doing that because you could not really understand and you thought it would not be proper. But it is Pippo's death that is not proper.

'I curse you, Matteo, because you are incapable of doing anything. Cullaccio's blood did not stain your shirt. I wanted you to recount how he had shouted and fought, and pleaded with you in vain to get you to stop. I wanted you to tell me all the little details. I hoped that would bring me some small, fragile solace, like a little breath of air on my wound. You brought me nothing but stammering excuses. I don't want your excuses. I don't want to begin to think that you are not up to the challenge and to despise you a little more with each passing week. The world is upside down, Matteo. And I thought that you would know how to make it right for me. But no, fathers are not strong any more. Sons die. And it is left to grieving mothers to cry with rage for what has been stolen from them. I curse you, Matteo, for the promise of vengeance you made me but then left behind on our dirty pavements.'

IX

The Ghosts of Avellino
(August 2002)

I've been driving for over an hour now. I've left Vesuvius and the Bay of Naples behind me. The motorway's practically empty. I'm speeding towards Bari, heading up into the mountains around Avellino, and the air pouring in through the two open windows is cooler than on the coast. Heading due east over the high craggy ground, I'll soon reach the modern buildings of Avellino. The town is the same age as me, born with the 1980 earthquake. This is where the tremors that devastated Naples and the whole of the Mezzogiorno started, where everything fell dead in a matter of seconds. I pass the exact epicentre of the blast that flattened every house for miles around. The whole place has been rebuilt in the same bland, characterless style, designed with only speed and functionality in mind. Nothing here is beautiful any more – it has lost its sheen. History was buried under the rubble. In the end, the charmless modernity of the place was the ugliest scar left by the disaster.

I cross the green hills of Avellino. I feel ashamed. I have always felt responsible for this tragedy. I can't tell anyone – they'd think I was mad – but is it really so impossible? Garibaldo's always repeating the story of Frederick II, as he heard it from the professor. If it's true, is it not possible that death was provoked by our affront? That day, it shook the earth with all its rage. It swallowed thousands of men, women and children, whole families caught without warning by a collapsing roof or wall. I know it was down to me. Death sought to punish us for our disobedience, to knock down the little men who had dared to defy it. It roared in outrage. A great cloud of dust spread from Naples to Avellino. From Caserta to Matera, the roads were crisscrossed with cracks, and they were the clefts left by death's anger.

I was born that night, going through my second birth while so many others were meeting their deaths. I screamed like a newborn. The air burnt my lungs a second time. A great roar responded to my cry. I was born, bringing tears and terror to the town.

A single quake was not enough for death. That night in Naples there were fifty-six aftershocks spreading through every part of the city, leaving cracks in the walls and uprooting the lamp posts. The Neapolitans spent the whole night making the sign of the cross, convinced they were all going to be consumed by the earth.

I've always had the feeling it was me who killed all those people. I carry the guilt with me. How could a life have come out of that? I can't sleep at night. It drives me mad. I'm jolted awake. At night, I hear the earthquake victims calling me, their big eyes and twisted features demanding to know why my life was worth more than theirs, what I've done to be saved while they were sacrificed.

I've never talked to anyone about the things I see. I wake with a start and lie there under the sheets, my skin pale and teeth chattering, knowing it's only a matter of time before the ghostly shadows are back and that the day is only a brief reprieve between nights. I must be mad. There's no way I could have gone through all this and not be. I grew up without a mother but it made no difference – I learnt to live without her. I'm going to find my father. I'm the only one who can. I'm young and strong. I know the way. I have the dust of the dead inside me. They'll recognise me and let me through. Maybe they'll even take me to my father – he won't have the strength to walk. I can't wait for him to cry on my shoulder and smile to see his son return.

X
The Grieving Mother's Notes
(September 1980)

Giuliana continued to work at the Grand Hotel Santa Lucia. She slept there as well. Giosuè had found her a place to stay. The first evening, when she had left Matteo, it was Giosuè she had gone to see. She had begged him to find her a corner where she could hide for a while. He had taken her to the basement and had shown her a little stockroom where boxes of soap and linen were stored. 'I can put a mattress in here,' he had said. 'The machines start early in the morning but you will have peace and quiet at night.'

She had been there a month. She worked hard. Asked for nothing. Never refused to do whatever was asked of her. As soon as she had some free time, she went out. She walked the streets of the city with an air of concentration. All she did was walk. And talk very quietly, battling the demons that accompanied her. She murmured prayers, stopped to cross herself, then set off again. In a few weeks, her appearance had changed. When she passed a church, she would stop dead, like someone searching for something that would be impossible to describe until they found it. Then she went on her way, head bent.

Finally, one day, when rain had driven people back to their homes and she was sheltering under a porch, her face lit up. She had found what she had been looking for all that time. She murmured to herself: 'The wall.' The idea grew in her.

'The wall, over there. They lean forward and kiss it. The wall receives their wishes and does not move. That's what I need.'

She took a scrap of paper from her bag and scribbled a few words. Then, in spite of the rain, which continued to beat down on the pavement, she went in search of a church. The first she found was San Domenico Maggiore. The square in front was empty. She stopped. She wanted to take her time. She went slowly over to the church and slipped her piece of paper into the crack between two stones then furtively kissed the façade, crossed herself and slipped away.

From that moment on, this was all she did. She roamed all over the city. As soon as she came across a church, she wrote on a scrap of paper, rolled it into a ball and slipped it into a cavity or between two stones. She always asked the same thing of the church façades. She asked for her son to be returned to her. One day soon. She asked for the blood and bereavement to be wiped away. Her ex-voto offerings multiplied day by day. Soon there were dozens and dozens of little balls of paper endlessly repeating the same plea, 'I'm waiting for my son.' Naples said nothing. The façades were mute. Sometimes the wind blew the little messages down. Sometimes the local children pulled one out and laughed as they read it. But, mostly, they remained half concealed in the stone, hidden supplications, like little eggs of pain.

Giuliana continued. Relentlessly. Everywhere she went. The words multiplied over the city. 'I'm waiting for my son.' She rolled the message into a ball and slipped it into San Gregorio Armeno. 'May Pippo be returned to me or may the world burn,' in Santa Maria Donnalbina. 'Don't make me the mother of a dead boy,' in San Giorgio Maggiore. 'You are cursed if my son does not return,' in Chiesa Madre. These were the words she slipped into the façades. So that the whole of Naples would have the same name on their lips. Pippo. Pippo. Pippo.

Because she was going from church to church she soon heard about Don Gaetano Marinucci. He was the young priest who had just been appointed at Santa Maria di Montesanto. Since his arrival, services were no longer poorly attended. The young priest was handsome. He had the rugged charisma of dark-eyed men. Like Giuliana, he came from Puglia. The rumour spread through the neighbourhood that the young priest had been a disciple of Padre Pio, and that he had accompanied him during his last years. His association with the holy man conferred an aura of glory on the young man. Most of the women in the fish markets of Montesanto were certain that, one day, the young priest would also perform miracles and become the worthy successor to Padre Pio. Now it was Naples' turn to have their saint and the entire world would see what the common people were capable of when they wished to demonstrate their fervour.

Giuliana wandered more and more often about the Montesanto neighbourhood. She walked around the church. Each time she passed in front of it, she deposited one of her little notes. So that after a few days there were many in the wall of the church. She wanted to cover the façade with them so that the priest would know that she was there and that she expected great things of him.

One night, she finally felt she was ready. She went to the church. It was about two in the morning. The sky was clear and the stars shone with the purity of the night. She knelt in front of the closed church door and murmured her exhortation.

'I kneel in front of you, Father, but do not think that I am weak. I am strong. I believe in you. You are going to perform a miracle for me and I can already feel joy spreading through my veins. I know that men like you are capable of such things. It is not that miracles are easy for them to perform. But their purpose here on earth is to relieve us of our misfortunes. I know what is coming. The blind will see. The paralysed will start to walk. I know all that. I am ready. It is time for the dead to be resurrected. All of them, one by one, will ascend from below the earth and walk. I wait impatiently. Maybe it cannot be seen as a miracle. Just the reconciliation between God and man. Because he has offended us. You know that as well as I do. Through Pippo's death, he threw me to the ground and beat me. It was an act of cruelty and I curse him for it. But today the hour of pardon has come. The Lord himself will kneel before us and ask our pardon. I will look at him for a long time, I will kiss his forehead and I will forgive him. And that is when the dead will rise, for it will be the end. It is good. I pray that day will come. I am full of strength. I will wait until tomorrow. I already feel the earth tremble. The dead are on the move. They are preparing and quivering with impatience. In only a few hours' time, the Lord will appear before us. I can't wait, my father, to see him kneeling in front of me and crying with humility.'

Early in the morning, she went to sit against the wall of the church, out of sight of the arriving worshippers. The bells pealed. Little by little the crowd in front of the church formed into small groups. Almost all women – the old women from the local area and shopkeepers going to mass before work. Giuliana did not get up. She did not mix with the crowd. She waited until everyone had gone in and mass had started. Then she went up the steps of the church and stood in the entrance watching the young priest. There he was, with the contemplative, austere demeanour she had imagined. She did not go in. 'I will not receive communion from the Lord until he has asked my pardon,' she thought. She did not feel hate. She was waiting until mass was finished, like a mother waiting for her child to charge out of school at the end of the day.

Finally, the organ rang out. One by one the women began to leave. Giuliana went in, pushing her way through the oncoming crowd. There were still about ten people standing in front of the altar. The priest was giving them the host. She stayed where she was, confident and at peace. 'The organ does not know it, but it is playing to celebrate this day,' she thought.

At last, the church was empty. Still she waited, in the last row of the pews, like a parishioner lost in contemplation. When they were really on their own she went straight up to him.

'Don Marinucci, I am Giuliana.'

He didn't say anything. He looked at her strangely, waiting

for her to explain, because he did not know who she was.

'You're going to perform a miracle,' she went on. 'I have come to tell you. Tell my son to walk, wherever he is, and he will walk again. It is time.'

The priest understood that she was a lost soul. He looked at her with sympathy and a gentle serenity as he took both her hands in his. 'What happened to your son?' he asked.

'He's dead,' she replied. 'Until yesterday. But that doesn't matter because God is going to ask my forgiveness. I will kiss his forehead and he will not be ashamed any more. The dead are going to come back.'

'What are you saying?' demanded the priest, his voice rising with fear.

So Giuliana explained that for weeks she had been putting bits of paper into the stone of his church to warn him. She spoke of Padre Pio's miracles, which were nothing compared to the miracles he was capable of. The people needed them. She repeated several times that the people were suffering and that it was God's fault. She explained everything that was in her head and she mentioned Pippo in almost every sentence, as if that would make him come more quickly. The priest's expression darkened. He looked at her, scandalised, and said severely, 'So it was you: all those little bits of paper?'

'Yes,' she replied. 'Today you are going to give me my son back.'

'Silence!' he said, raising his voice, looking disgusted. 'You should be ashamed of yourself and your superstitions. You have blasphemed. You dare to insult the Lord. You challenge His authority. Your child is with Him. He stands on His right-hand side. He has welcomed him into the light. And you want Him to ask for pardon …'

At these words, Giuliana took a step backwards and spat at the feet of the priest. He blanched and swiftly slapped her. The sound of the smack echoed in the empty church.

'These are Pharisaic beliefs,' continued the priest. 'Tomorrow I will burn all your notes. God does not ask pardon. He took your son back. That was His wish and we must praise Him ...'

Giuliana could not stand any more. The priest's words grated on her. He appeared to be laughing at her with the cruelty of a devil. She began to scream. A shrill scream that lasted a long time and seemed to split the still air of the church. She screamed and birds all over the neighbourhood flew away. Then, before the priest could say another word, she left.

A few hours later she was at Naples station. She had gone back to the Grand Hotel Santa Lucia to collect her belongings, then she had walked through the streets of the city for the last time. On the station concourse, all she had was her suitcase and the ticket she had just bought. She was no more than a shadow, a poor shadow who got into the first train that came, going to Caserta.

'At Naples station I abandon my child.'

The train had just moved off. Giuliana was looking out of the window. There were still some people left on the sad-looking platform, waiting to say goodbye to those leaving. She stared at these last faces and thought back over the life she had spent in that city, the life she was leaving behind her, and which did not now exist for anyone except Matteo. She would never return. Her son would stay, buried in the cemetery. Her life as a mother was over. She leant her forehead against the window and said goodbye to the thousand things that made up Pippo's life. His school. His bedroom. His clothes: the ones he liked, the ones he never wore. She said goodbye to the joy of going out with him, of holding his hand in hers. She said goodbye to the maternal worry that had overtaken her from pregnancy onwards and that should have stayed with her all her life. One last time, she extracted him from the cold marble of his grave so that she could hear him laugh. He was there. He was playing with her. He was calling her as he ran. She closed her eyes so that they were on their own and she was everything to him.

At Naples station, she laughed for one last time with her son. She knew it would never happen again and she tried to make her last maternal laughter go on as long as possible.

'At Naples station, I abandoned my child,' she murmured, 'and I will never think of him again.'

The train travelled along the track with the heaviness of

sleepless nights. She was in no hurry, in no rush to arrive anywhere. She was saying goodbye to her life. Every new station was a step on the way to its slow, progressive dissolution.

At Caserta, where, despite the late hour, the platform was packed with people laden with luggage and children, she said goodbye to Matteo. She was leaving behind her husband, who had only been able to offer her gifts that fate had destroyed. A life built on sand and swept away in an instant. Everything had been gobbled up. At Caserta she kissed Matteo in her thoughts for the last time before the train moved off again.

At Benevento, she understood that she would not be able to take any memories with her. The platform was empty. They stayed a strangely long time in the station even though no one got on or off. The carriage doors had not even opened. Perhaps the train had simply stopped for so long in order to give her time to abandon everything. For at Benevento she left behind all her memories. Every single one. They were scattered like a photo album that had been shaken out of the window. She sprinkled them over the platform. Twenty years of memories she would have no use for any more. The hours spent in the hotel doing the same things over and over again. Cleaning. Washing. Serving. Happy moments. The surprises that should have gladdened her heart right into old age. Everything, she was leaving everything. She shook out her memory like shaking out a tablecloth and eventually the train set off again.

At Foggia, it was all finished. She got up, took her suitcase and opened the door. It must have been two in the morning. She was surprised because it was pleasant outside despite the late hour. She got off the train. She did not raise her head, tried not to take in the station. She walked with lowered head.

'My name is Giuliana Mascheroni,' she said under her breath, and she repeated her old name, given to her by her father, so that it would become second nature. Her old name from before her marriage, the name from the period before her life had started and when she had been eager for everything. She leant forward to take up this old name, as if she were picking up something she had left behind twenty years ago.

'My name is Giuliana Mascheroni. My life has not started yet. I am my parents' daughter. Nothing more. And I have come back to die in the place where I was born.'

XI
Overwhelming
(August 2002)

The blood on the seat next to me has dried. The scent of pine hits me out of the darkness. I drive on. The cool breeze keeps me awake. The night is doing me good. I look around. There's an innocent freshness in the air of the hills.

I can't get Grace's voice out of my head. I shouldn't have gone to see her. I'm annoyed with myself for having felt the need to say goodbye. I should have been stronger. I'm a bundle of nerves and rage. I expected Grace to stroke my hand and give me her blessing – instead, she's planted an idea I can't shake off. But I mustn't allow myself to give in. Not now.

I'm thinking of my mother. I can't help it. I wish I could get her out of my mind but she sneaks back in, overwhelming me, and Grace's voice is there too, telling me over and over again that my mother has been in hell for twenty years. She's not the one I'm looking for. She's not the one I'm driving towards. I need to ignore that idea.

My mother doesn't exist. I can't picture her face. However far back I go, I can't remember a mother's soothing, gentle presence. Or maybe I can. Deep down I know I once had a mother, but I've pushed her away. I do remember her. If I make an effort, I can remember a time when she was there, surrounding me with the sweet scent of happiness. And then, just like that, she was gone. My mother left, abandoning her son. That, I remember – the sudden emptiness. I never crossed her mind again for a second. She made up her mind never to think of me again. And so I did the same. When I became aware she had banished me from her thoughts, I swore I would never long for her, hope for her, cherish her, ever again.

Just when I needed her most, she shrank away from me. What kind of mother does that? I could tell what my parents were thinking – the warmth of their affection was all I had to keep me going. I could feel my father's obsession with reliving the day of the shooting, feel him praying to hold me in his arms one last time. For a long time I could feel her too, refusing to accept my death, and then she disappeared and I never entered her mind again. What kind of mother does that? She left. She wiped my name and my very existence from her memory and left me limping along without a mother's support. I needed her. I was lonely, I cried out for her. I needed her to help me keep the shadows away and hold back my oblivion. I needed her, a child trapped in a terrifying place with no way out. I called her name, over and over. It made no difference. I begged her to come back, to let me feel the warmth of her thoughts again. Nothing. In the end, I managed to cut away the pain. I clung to my father. I could feel him in his grief, thinking of me every second of every day. I could feel him getting closer to me, and it was the only thing that kept the ghouls and the screeching spirits at bay.

I have no mother. Grace was wrong. I have no mother who has thought of me the way a mother should think of her child. But there's still this word, which goes round and round for ever, this overwhelming word which causes me pain. My mother.

XII
The Dead around the Table
(November 1980)

Matteo had been driving for more than two hours through the sleeping city. He was thinking about Giuliana, whom he had not heard from. He thought about the boredom that was crushing the life out of him. He drove along Via Cristofo Colombo by the sea. The streets were empty. When he turned the corner onto Via Melisurgo, he passed a pedestrian who looked familiar. He observed the man in his rear-view mirror, certain he had met him at some point. It took him a while to realise that it was Professore Provolone, whom he had come across in Grace's café a few weeks earlier. What was he doing here in the middle of nowhere at this hour? Without thinking, Matteo swung his car round.

He retraced his route to be sure of finding him. A few minutes later he saw him disappearing at the end of the road into a little recess. Matteo parked the car to follow him on foot.

When he reached the spot he had seen the large flabby figure of the professor disappearing into, he heard voices. He immediately felt that something was wrong and quickened his pace. Laughter could be heard in the dark. When he was close enough, he could make out three young boys laughing and kicking a form on the ground. It could only be the professor. The three thugs were hitting him with an innocence that was almost joyful, as if they were kicking a cardboard carton or an old wooden box. Matteo heard groans coming from the body. Suddenly one of the youths undid his fly and pissed on his victim, looking triumphant.

Matteo shouted and ran straight at the attackers. The boys did not seem afraid. The one who had urinated did himself up slowly and asked insolently, 'What do you want?'

'Leave him alone,' replied Matteo, putting up his fists in case they attacked him.

The three young people looked at each other, amused. 'You want your turn too?' one of them asked.

'We won't charge you,' said the third, laughing.

'Leave him alone,' repeated Matteo through gritted teeth.

The youngsters seemed to hesitate, as if wondering if it would be worth taking him on. They were weighing their desire to fight against the fatigue or amusement that would result. Finally, one of the boys said, 'Take him and bugger off, or we'll piss on you too!'

The little group laughed cruelly. '*Eh, professore!* We'll carry on whenever you like!' cried the biggest boy. They bumped shoulders and gave the body on the ground a last kick. Then they turned and left. As they were going, Matteo heard them laughing like kids after a football game. They shouted and gesticulated with arrogance and pride.

'*Professore?*' said Matteo, hurrying over to him.

Provolone was lying on his side. His flaccid penis hung out of his open fly. His shirt was stained with urine and his face was beaten up. His mouth was bleeding and his upper lip swollen. When Matteo leant over him and said his name softly, he was surprised to see that he seemed to be laughing.

'*Professore? Professore?* Are you all right?'

The professor did not reply. He continued to smile and murmur as if in a fever.

'*Professore?* Stand up. I'll help you.'

The man gripped Matteo's arm and got up, saying, 'I tell you, angels in the sky … if they exist … could not be more beautiful than those three hooligans! …'

Matteo found this strange but did not reply. He thought the man was delirious and confused by the shock of the attack.

'I have my car nearby,' he said, helping the injured man to walk. 'Lean on me.'

All the time they were hobbling along, Provolone was laughing and murmuring, 'Bless them! The rascals, bless them! For kicking me like that! Beasts! That's what they were: ravishing beasts!'

Matteo opened the door of the café with one hand. With the other, he made sure that the professor was able to follow him. As soon as he entered he was greeted with a joyous 'There he is! It's my driver!'

Grace was there, like the last time, sipping a cocktail and pouting like an American starlet.

'What happened?' asked Garibaldo as soon as he saw Provolone's bleeding face.

'He was attacked,' replied Matteo, helping Provolone to sit at a table. 'I brought him here so that he could have a restorative drink.'

'And I thank you …' stammered the professor, 'really … Thank you … but you mustn't … in any way … I've been a terrible nuisance …'

Garibaldo had brought over an ice bucket, a clean cloth and a bottle of grappa that he put on the table.

'Did they steal anything from you?' asked Matteo.

Strangely, he heard Grace choking with laughter behind him, as if it was a stupid question. The professor blushed and replied, 'I'm very grateful for your concern … I really am … But everything is fine … I'm sorry to have involved you in all this …'

Grace winked mockingly at Matteo and, when he seemed not to understand, said, 'What the *professore* means is that it wasn't a fight you interrupted but a form of flirting!'

Matteo was astounded. He looked at the man he had just

brought in to see whether he would confirm or deny this and the professor said with an embarrassed little shrug, 'I understand why you were mistaken … I really do …'

'But …' Matteo was having trouble believing it.

'Yes,' Provolone went on. 'What can I say … I love those little street urchins … I really do … I just can't help myself …'

Grace burst out laughing. She raised her glass and said, 'To Professore Provolone!'

Matteo remained stunned for some time. He didn't know whether to laugh or to be annoyed. There was something going on here that he did not understand. 'The world is upside down,' he thought and he drank the glass of grappa Garibaldo was holding out to him with a smile.

'If there's anything I can do …' replied Provolone. 'Really … I'm so embarrassed.'

Matteo looked at him in amazement. He just could not understand how anyone could choose to be attacked for pleasure. He did not ask the question but his confusion must have been obvious because the professor lowered his eyes and tried to explain. 'You're wondering why I do it, aren't you? … I imagine that's what you're thinking … You remember the conversation we had last time? About death living in us … The feeling of being a ghost sometimes … Yes, exactly that … A ghost … Without life … In those moments, you see, when they hit me and laugh so savagely, when I feel their glorious muscles on me … I come alive. Strange to relate. But I assure you. I feel, yes, there's no other way of saying it … vividly alive …'

Matteo said nothing. He thought back to the conversation they had had when they first met. 'Why did you say that life and death were more entwined than people think?'

The professor passed his hand over his face, smiled gently and replied, 'Because it's true ... People today are rational and unimaginative and they believe that there is an absolute barrier between the two, but nothing could be further from the truth. We are not either alive or dead. Not in any way ... It is much more complicated than that. Everything is muddled up and layered. The Ancients knew that. The world of the living and that of the dead overlap. There are bridges, intersections, grey areas. We have simply stopped knowing how to see them and feel them.'

Grace and Garibaldo were listening intently, and, seeing that the conversation was becoming serious, the owner of the café decided to lay a table and invited his guests to make themselves at home. He brought four glasses, a bottle and two fine *mozzarelle di bufala*. Then he went to close the door to indicate that he did not want to be disturbed by any more customers who might come and interrupt the intimacy of their little gathering.

Grace smiled. The night was going to belong to them. They were all united in their desire just to listen to each other, not to have to worry about the present and to have a break from the outside world.

'And why do you believe the frontier between life and death is so porous?' demanded Garibaldo, biting into a *tramezzino* with ham and artichokes. Before opening the bar and enjoying the camaraderie of the café, he had been active in movements of the extreme left, and he approached everything concerning the afterlife with profound suspicion.

'Have you lost someone close to you?' asked Provolone.

Garibaldo said nothing but he was thinking about his girlfriend who had died ten years earlier of a galloping cancer.

'Don't you ever have the feeling that they live on in you? Honestly ... That they have left behind something in you that will not disappear until you yourself die? Gestures, maybe, or a way of speaking or thinking. A loyalty to certain things and places, perhaps. Believe me. The dead live. They make us do certain things. They influence our decisions and behaviour. They shape us.'

'Yes,' replied Grace bitterly. 'That's when there is still something to shape.'

'Exactly!' exclaimed the professor jubilantly. 'That's the other side of the porosity between the two worlds. Sometimes we are barely alive ourselves. When the dead leave, they take away a little piece of us too. Each bereavement progressively kills us. We've all had experience of that. Our joy and light diminish with each bereavement ... We die a little bit more each time as we lose those around us.'

Matteo said nothing and gritted his teeth.

'Really, that is why ...' the professor went on, 'I say that the two states overlap. Look around Naples, on certain evenings; wouldn't you say it feels as if it's full of shadows?'

Matteo smiled. How many times had he felt that as he drove around the deserted streets of the city? How many times had it seemed as if he were in a strange suspended world?

A sudden noise interrupted Matteo's thoughts and caused them all to jump at the same time. Then they looked around. At first they thought someone was knocking at the door but that was not it. The hammerings grew louder and Matteo was about to get up and go and see whether a drunkard had decided to try to beat the wall down with his fists, when Garibaldo cried, 'It's Mazerotti, the priest!' He immediately sprang out of his chair and hurried over to the window. Matteo watched his agitation in amazement. He didn't understand what was going on. Garibaldo was closing the shutters, exactly as if he needed to hide urgently. Why was he barricading himself in like that? Was he on such bad terms with the priest that he wanted to keep him out of his establishment? Matteo was turning this over in his mind, still not understanding, when he saw Garibaldo leaning over a trapdoor in the floor that led to the stockroom. He opened it, murmuring, 'I'm coming, I'm coming.' That's when Matteo realised that the priest was in the cellar and had been knocking on the trapdoor.

'But ...' he asked, taken aback, 'you leave him down there?'

'No!' replied Grace, laughing. 'Mazerotti dug a passage from the crypt of the church to the café cellar. That way, he doesn't have to cross the road.'

'But why?' asked Matteo, more and more confused by what was happening around him.

Grace didn't have time to reply. The trapdoor opened completely and the head of an emaciated old man appeared.

'You took your time about it,' he said sounding like an old woman.

When the priest was on his feet, and in the middle of the room, Garibaldo closed the trapdoor, again stirring up a cloud of dust. Matteo was able to watch the old man closely. He must have been in his seventies, dried up and so wrinkled he looked as gnarled as the wooden stick he carried over his arm. He was as toothless as a beggar and his eyes were ruined – the left one squinted wildly, the right was veiled by a cataract, which gave him the look of an ancient tortoise.

'Sit down, Don Mazerotti,' said Grace, gently. She was, of all of them there, the one who knew the old man best. Truth to tell, she would have given her life for this old scrap of humanity, who for years had listened to her, counselled her, sometimes reprimanded her, but had always been in her life without ever heaping opprobrium on her, even when she talked of the nights she prostituted herself at the port, the bodies she sucked on filthy summer nights, or the boorish men who took her so roughly she cried and then left her distraught, on her knees, on the ground in an alley picking up two ten-thousand-lire notes before blowing her nose and putting her stockings back on. She told him everything: the sadness that sometimes overwhelmed her, feeling like a freak when local children followed her, calling out, 'Poofter! Poofter!', not knowing exactly what they were saying but happy to see that the word chased her away.

'Why does he come here in secret?' Matteo asked Garibaldo.

'He's afraid that Vatican envoys will take advantage of a moment when he's not there to take over his church.'

'They would do that?'

'Yes,' murmured Garibaldo with a conspiratorial air, and he explained to Matteo that, as the years had gone by, the church of Santa Maria del Purgatorio had attracted all the misfits of the night. Tramps, prostitutes and the mentally ill came to pray at the church. Don Mazerotti welcomed them all and celebrated mass with them in the usual way. The clergy had come to see this as a provocation. They thought Don Mazerotti was teaching them a lesson. In opening his doors to these broken, dirty, stinking souls, he was underlining the behaviour of the well-off in other churches, and declaring loud and clear that he was the only one to tend to the common people of Naples. Relations had become antagonistic. No one wanted a communist priest right in the middle of Spaccanapoli. One day, the clerical authorities had demanded that Mazerotti give up his church and go and join the nearby monastery. He refused. Tensions worsened. The authorities sent a second letter, then a third. They threatened him with excommunication if he refused. Mazerotti did not give in. That was why he barricaded himself in. He no longer went out, he locked the door and only agreed to receive the few regulars who wanted to have their confession heard. He came to Garibaldo to eat, always passing through the tunnel so that no one saw him. The locals had nicknamed him '*il matto*' and there was not a day that went by without women leaving baskets of food or a few bottles on the steps of the church, which the old man would fetch in after nightfall, like a wary cat.

Don Mazerotti sat down and looked at the men around him.

'I've interrupted you,' he said with a courtesy that appeared at odds with his scrawny appearance.

'Not at all,' said Grace.

'The *professore* was explaining that we are all more dead than we think,' added Matteo.

'That is so true,' replied the priest.

At that moment Garibaldo raised his hands to stop the conversation and prevent his guests from embarking on a lengthy discussion.

'Wait. Wait,' he said hospitably. He felt as if he had gone back in time to the days when, with a few friends, he prepared for the revolution in smoke-filled cellars. 'I'll make us something to eat, and then we'll resume. What would you like?'

It was decided that they would have a lovely onion frittata and pappardelle with porcini. Garibaldo felt the circumstances were exceptional and warranted a meal on the house. Very soon, the delicious smell of frying mushrooms rose from the kitchens.

For the first time in a long while Matteo felt happy. He looked at his strange companions: a disgraced professor, a transvestite, a mad priest and the easy-going owner of a café. He wanted to share a meal with these men, to listen to what they had to say, to stay with them in the dim light of the little room, far from the world and his grief.

'So you also think we are more dead than alive?'

Garibaldo asked the priest the question between two mouthfuls. He was looking at him with the curiosity of a child.

'After forty years of hearing confession, I'm certain of it,' replied the old man mischievously. 'You wouldn't believe the number of parishioners I have listened to for whom life really is nothing any more. They don't even realise it, but all they talk about are their little fears and habits. Nothing is meaningful for them. Nothing moves them or stirs them up. Their days just follow on from each other. There is no life in all that. They are shadows. Nothing but shadows. For forty years, I have seen them pass through my confessional. Most don't have very much to say. They feel weighed down by problems but have none to recount. No violent desire, no crime, no internal turmoil. Just some dirty little acts. Luckily the body grows old!'

Matteo looked at Grace. She was smiling sadly. Something in her face had changed. It had become a mask of terrifying sadness. What kind of life does she lead? wondered Matteo. Was she really as happy as she seemed when she was talking excitedly and gesticulating, or were her days an endless succession of disappointments? In fact, were any of them round the table fully alive?

'I absolutely agree,' said the professor, smiling at the priest. 'Without having your experience of confession, of course, I can speak … it's true … only for me … If we are a little bit honest with ourselves … isn't it … an obvious fact …'

'And there was I thinking you were going to try to sell me the idea of eternal paradise and peace for our souls,' said Garibaldo, drinking a glass of grappa. 'I think I would actually have preferred that, because what you are saying is so sad and depressing!'

'Do you know the hypogeum of Ħal Saflieni? In Malta?' asked the professor suddenly, of no one in particular, as if Garibaldo had not spoken. 'No? It's a magnificent example of the porosity of the two worlds. In Valletta, you can visit the immense underground chambers dating back to around 3000 BC. There is a succession of caves and cellars. No one knows much about the people who built the catacombs. But I found an interesting document on the subject. There was a Polish researcher at the beginning of the twentieth century who had a fascinating theory: according to him, the building of the catacombs was the first mass rebellion against death.'

'What does that mean?' demanded Grace, lighting a cigarette.

'According to the Pole, the giant underground chambers were built so that people could live closer to their dead,' replied the professor. 'Everyone including women and children went to live underground. In a labyrinth of underground caves, to be closer to their lost loved ones. The people of Malta rejected mourning.'

'Where are these caves?' Garibaldo was amazed by what he was hearing.

'On the outskirts of Valletta. But Malta is full of underground caverns from different eras. Near Mdina there are the catacombs of St Paul and of St Agatha. It's as if people on Malta have always wanted to live close to their dead.'

'Incredible!' exclaimed the old priest.

Garibaldo got up to open the trapdoor the priest had come up through a few hours earlier, and went down to the cellar. He could be heard breathing heavily. There was the sound of objects being dragged across the floor, then two arms reappeared and deposited a box on the stone floor, creating a cloud of dust. The large man then extricated himself fully from the trapdoor and put the box down by the table. He opened it with a knife and took all the bottles out at once – three in each hand – and deposited them on the table, like trophies, saying triumphantly, 'They're not as old as the subterranean caves of Malta, but they have lived longer than any of us.'

They were six dusty bottles of a Neapolitan wine as thick as buffalo blood and black as the tears that flow down the cheeks of the porcelain Madonna of Castelfiorito on every 24 April.

'How will I be able to go to work after drinking all that?' asked Grace, pretending to be outraged. 'Even those kinky Albanian sailors will be scared off!' she added and everyone laughed heartily.

'Tonight,' replied the priest, 'is not about working, it's about learning.' And he added with the glee of an old man who takes pleasure in being scandalous, 'You can get up to your dirty stuff tomorrow. And don't worry about the Albanian sailors, they'll find other mouths to empty themselves into!'

The little group was momentarily taken aback, astonished to hear a man of the church speak so crudely. But Grace, who was a bit drunk, giggled, and the others followed suit, laughing along at the salacious words of this priest who was old enough to be pope but talked like a lowlife from the northern districts of Naples.

'If you will permit me, there is better yet,' said the professor, delighted to have won over his audience, who were now ready to let him talk for hours. 'Do you know the Fayum portraits?'

Only Garibaldo nodded. So the professor tried to describe to the others the strange intensity of the faces from the first or second century AD. Noblemen, peasants, women and young shepherds, all gazing directly out of the portraits with round eyes, for all eternity.

'There have been numerous theories about the meaning of these portraits,' he said. 'Some say they are mortuary portraits intended to be placed on catafalques. And that the faces have been looking at us since their deaths. That is both true and false. It is more complicated than that. In AD 55 the Nile flooded badly. A few days before, a young shepherd had predicted that the river would burst its banks and he had tried, in vain, to warn the villagers nearby. He was only believed by a group of young people his age, who left the area to seek shelter. The day of the catastrophe, everything was swept away in minutes. The river swallowed everything. An enormous wave of mud devoured the houses, the animals and the people. Everything was wiped out. When the survivors returned to their villages a few days later, the river had gone down to its normal level but there was nothing else left. Where houses had been, there was now nothing but mud. That very evening great funeral celebrations took place. And that was when something incredible happened: the dead came back, slowly walking out of the waters. They took their place amongst the living, sang with them, danced with them. All around there were tears and reunions. Later in the night when the moon had disappeared behind clouds, the dead copulated with the living. They stole a last embrace from fate that had separated them with such violence. Widows found their husbands. Young dead men

112

embraced the young farm girls they had promised to marry when they were alive. Children were born of that improbable night. And they were strange beings – pale shadows who did not speak. And they are the ones who are represented in the Fayum portraits. They were painted so that the world would know what had happened on the banks of the Nile. So that the world would know that, here, men had vanquished death and the anger of the river.'

No one around the little table moved. Grace and the priest sat like children drinking in the professor's words. Matteo was in turmoil, overcome by emotion. His jaw was clenched and his eyes lowered. The professor's story had plunged him back into his personal grief. It was all there again. He had a sad feeling of powerlessness and horrible resignation. As though he had just put on a big stinking overcoat and everything around him was once again unbearable and nauseating. His face darkened. He downed his glass of wine, but it did not help. The wine had a bitter taste, which made him regret finishing it. He was overwhelmed by visions of his son. He saw Pippo lying in the ambulance; Pippo running behind him trying not to be late; Pippo moaning because his father was hurting his wrist.

'So nowadays how would you make the dead rise again?' he asked quietly.

The others looked embarrassed. They all knew what he was referring to. They were worried he would break down and wail like a madman or cry into his glass.

'I don't know,' the professor replied calmly.

Matteo smiled sardonically. So everything the professor had said before was just words.

'You made it all up,' said Matteo, staring at the floor. 'The dead do not rise again, *professore*.'

'No, indeed, they don't,' he replied, still very calm. 'But you can descend.'

Matteo looked at him, stupefied. He was going to ask 'Descend where?' But he did not. Because he knew that he had understood. The professor had meant descend down there. Into the Underworld. That was what the professor was saying. So why did he not burst out laughing or get annoyed at this unkind joke? Why was he still sitting there, turning the words over in his mind as if they were worth taking seriously? The three men with him were similarly still. None of them were the least surprised, or trying to suppress laughter. None of them seemed to consider it an idiotic proposition. Why? Had they all gone mad, hypnotised by the storyteller who was still looking seriously at them, awaiting their reply?

Then, into the semi-darkness, Matteo spoke. He did not speak to express shock at what the professor had suggested, nor to make fun of him. He did not smile sadly and say goodbye to them all; he did not tell the professor to shut up; he did not simply shrug wearily. No, instead he heard himself ask: 'How?' As if it were perfectly possible – as if they could seriously think of such an undertaking, and the only impediment to the project would be finding the means to carry it out.

He saw from the way the professor looked at him that he had been expecting that question. He had barely spoken when the professor got up to fetch an old leather satchel from the table. He opened it in front of the expectant group and brought out a pile of notes yellowed by time and entirely covered with frantic black handwriting. It all looked like some notebooks that had been torn apart by a mad person. Ten years of notes scribbled feverishly in dim libraries all over southern Italy.

He meticulously unpacked a massive jumble of scribbled-on papers, torn pages and annotated cards and showed them to his companions with the manic look of someone unveiling his secrets.

XIII
The Forgotten Gate of Naples
(November 1980)

'I know exactly what you are thinking, I really do; I've often encountered that look in the eyes of those who listen to me … believe me,' said the professor with a grin. 'I know. I'm mad. Making things up. Everyone tells me that. But you are wrong … I'm not inventing what I'm about to tell you. Not at all. I have simply unearthed it. We no longer believe in anything. And in order not to depress ourselves we call that progress. The Ancients left us traces of what they found. Maps. Texts. Objects. Representations. Researchers and university professors study and translate them, they analyse and comment on them, but, deep down, none of them believe what the papers tell us.'

Matteo and Garibaldo lowered their eyes. They wondered whether the professor was about to embark on a tale of woe. He must have felt that because he stopped dead, looked at his friends and when he began to speak again, it was to explain more clearly: 'There are several entrances to the Underworld.'

Now the men around the table were more attentive.

'They have always been there,' the old man went on. 'Particularly here, in the south of Italy. In ancient times everyone knew about them and no one found it incongruous. Here. Look at this map. It dates from the Greek period. Lake Avernus, a few miles from Naples, was a designated gate. For centuries, birds who flew over it died of asphyxiation from the gas emanating from the water. The lake was an entrance, then it seems death decided to seal it up and to open another one elsewhere. The same goes for Solfatara. I have been there. There is still a strong odour of sulphur and yellow earth which stinks of rotten eggs and takes you by the throat. These are undeniable signs that this was once an entrance to the world down below. And there are others. I have them all listed. Càlena Abbey. The catacombs at Palermo, before the Sicilians stored an entire population of skeletons dressed in fine clothes there. The mysterious underground caverns in Malta. The Sassi di Matera. There are many. It took me two years to draw up my map of the gates to the Underworld. I have it here. Look.'

The friends were staggered at this but leant forward to look at the sheet the old man was holding out. It was a map of southern Italy, dotted here and there with little marks around certain place names.

'What is that?' asked Matteo, pointing a finger at a little black circle on the map at the port of Naples.

'That's a gate,' the professor replied seriously.

'Here? In Naples?'

'Yes,' said the old man. 'That's the one we should try. No one knows it's there. There is a chance that it is still open. The others, on the other hand, must have been sealed up long ago.'

'But …' Garibaldo looked up at the professor warily as if he now did fear the man was mad. He couldn't finish his sentence and none of the others would ever know what it was he wanted to say because he was interrupted by Mazerotti, who straightened up suddenly with the solemn air of someone in command. They all jumped. Mazerotti had remained silent for most of the evening, his eyes half closed, leaning back slightly in his chair, which made everyone think he had fallen asleep, unsurprisingly considering his age and the alcohol they had consumed. They were wrong. The priest had not missed a word of what had been said. And, if he had remained quiet and still, it was because what the professor said had thrown him into deep confusion. The more the scholar spoke, the more the feeling grew in the priest that he been waiting his whole life for this moment. For years now he had been sceptical of Christian iconography and he no longer believed in the three-way division of the Hereafter. He had stopped talking about his flock in paradise or in purgatory and his heart had filled with a bored weariness. That evening, the professor's account rekindled his desire to believe.

Now he was sitting up in his chair, his face determined, his demeanour commanding, and he said in a voice that made the others tremble: 'I am old, ravaged for years by a malignant cancer which makes me shit blood. I'm going to die one day soon in that church I have had to barricade like a fortress because those dogs at the Vatican don't like the look of my parishioners. I can't bear the idea of waiting for my illness finally to consume me. I'm going to go down. I think that makes sense. And someone has to go and see what's down there.'

'Then two of us will go,' said Matteo.

Matteo could not stop thinking about what Giuliana had told him that fateful day: 'Bring Pippo back to me, or, if you can't, at least bring me the head of the man who killed him.' He had immediately opted for vengeance, believing that was the only course open to him, but this evening, in the company of these strange people, it seemed possible to envisage the other option. 'Bring Pippo back to me,' she had said. He had decided he would. He would descend to the Underworld. To see Pippo and bring him back. Or, at least, to ask his forgiveness and hold him again.

'If we go down,' said the priest, pouring himself more wine, 'it has to be this evening. I'm so far gone, I'm not sure I'll survive the night. With all I've drunk I wouldn't be surprised if my arteries exploded one by one. It's this evening or never.'

'What about us?' asked Grace, sounding anxious.

'You'll come with us as far as the gate and wait,' replied the priest.

'It's no use everyone going down,' added the professor, who could see that Grace was torn between her fear and the desire to show solidarity. 'In any case we'll probably be driven back ...'

'Why?' asked Garibaldo, intrigued by this new information.

'If there is too much life in us, the door won't open. You have to have enough death inside you to pass through.'

'In that case,' replied Garibaldo, who had obviously decided not to go down, 'we'll wait until you come up again. But before you go, I'll make you coffee ...'

And he hurried behind the counter.

The friends sat down again patiently. They heard jars opening, and then drawers, and the coffee grinder being switched on, then grinding and mixing. It was like listening to an alchemist on the verge of finding the secret of the philosopher's stone. Then, after a good ten minutes, Garibaldo reappeared with a little round tray bearing two cups of coffee. It smelt strange – a mixture of sweet liqueur and bitterness. Many different ingredients could be detected – jasmine, myrtle, lemon – but as if they had all been mixed with the smell of burning. Matteo looked into his cup – the coffee was red.

'Coffee for death,' said Garibaldo seriously. 'To keep you awake until you're in the Hereafter.'

The two men downed their coffee in one. Matteo immediately felt that the effects of the alcohol had been swept away. His senses had been slightly dulled and his thinking clouded, but now a powerful heat coursed through his veins.

'If I survive the coffee,' said the old priest, getting his breath back, 'it's because the worms aren't ready for me yet.'

The friends stood up. Matteo was alert and prepared. He felt strong. And resolute. The fresh evening wind stinging his cheeks did him good. Nothing could make him change his mind. Not the slightly grotesque appearance of their little group, nor the incongruous sight of the professor, who had just unfolded a map to direct them through the little streets. The sea breeze carried a humidity that made their skin slightly sticky.

'If I don't come back,' thought Matteo, 'at least my life will end on a beautiful night.'

The little group set off. Don Mazerotti moved slowly. Grace gave her arm to the old man so that he would not stumble on the dark cobblestones. Everything was silent and strange. Everywhere they went they disturbed large cats which ran off into the nearest heap of refuse or disappeared under cars. The pavements in the little backstreets of the city were strewn with rubbish. The people living in the neighbourhood piled it there in the evening without thinking about the overpowering, nauseating smell that it produced. The city slept in this stink of vomit and fried fish, like a guest who had fallen asleep at the table he was dining at, his cheek inches from his dirty plate.

Soon they left behind the narrow streets of Spaccanapoli and started down the wide avenues which led to the port. There were no cars. Everywhere was empty. Matteo looked at the city in astonishment. He knew it by heart. He had so often driven around it at that late hour, but tonight everything seemed different and strange. They were on foot, going at the halting rhythm of pilgrims lost in a strange land. They were a tight little group of men feeling their way in the night, like blind men holding each other by the arm or the shoulder so as not to get lost. Or like madmen in a boat gliding silently through the water, wide-eyed at a world they did not understand.

Soon they arrived at Castel Nuovo and turned left along Via Nuova Marina, the long avenue which bordered the sea. They walked on the left-hand pavement, with cars passing in both directions between them and the port. The professor was staggering a little and Garibaldo wondered if that was because he was weakened by his wounds or because of all the alcohol he had drunk.

Finally they arrived at the square where the church of Santa Maria del Carmine was situated, a large, dark and melancholy place, which opened onto the sea on one side. During the day it was both a market and car park. But at this hour of night it was inhabited by the ugly and the lame. Famished and ghostly shadows seeking drunkenness or sex appeared from everywhere. It was here that Grace came to work most of the time. Transvestites and prostitutes shared the space, each in their own corner, welcoming the wrecks of humanity who went from one group to the other according to what they were after and how desperate they were. Here was the prostitution of the poor, a far cry from the traditional brothels of the Spanish Quarter, or the exotic establishments of the Vomero. Here the bodies touching each other were half aroused, half sickened, and the notes that they gave in exchange were as torn and dirty as the hands that took them.

As soon as they appeared, the little group aroused malicious interest. Hoping for money, hunched, limping figures approached from all sides, wanting to feel them, sniff them, push them, steal from them, take everything from them, then leave them behind like emptied handbags abandoned on the pavement.

But as soon as they recognised Grace, they stepped back and let them pass. She kept them at a distance, scolding them and addressing them by name. 'Naza, you pig, get back, we're almost suffocating from your smell! And you, Dino, let the gentlemen through. You'd make a rat vomit with those eyes of yours!'

And when that was not enough, she went on to humiliate them by revealing their secrets. 'Raf, you cretin, do you want me to tell everyone what you like me to do to you on summer evenings?'

She spoke to them as if they were dogs, picking on them one by one, and that worked. They stayed at a distance long enough for them to reach the other side of the square.

'Over there! Over there!' said the professor, pointing at the sea.

'There's nothing there,' replied Garibaldo.

It was true. Once across Via Nuova Marina there was nothing but a little central reservation littered with empty cans, broken syringes and slumped men and then the metal gates protecting the entrance to the port.

'The towers!' said the professor, signalling they should cross.

On the central reservation which separated the two lanes of traffic there was indeed a truncated but wide little tower. Then beyond the second lane, at the foot of the gates to the harbour master's office, there was another one. They were ugly. Probably from ancient times, but so patched up with brick that they looked totally ordinary. Like a pair of warts.

When they crossed over and reached the first reservation, it was like being on a little island, in the midst of the two lanes of traffic, fast-moving at this time of day.

'That's it! That's it!' the professor kept repeating, pointing at the tower.

Garibaldo and Matteo went over and immediately tried to clear a way through the wild grasses, brambles and hollyhocks clogging up the entrance. Then they pushed the door, which yielded with just a tired creaking of rotten wood. Cold air came up the stairs as though from a grotto or sarcophagus.

'Let's go,' said Mazerotti, without the slightest hesitation and with an energy no one had thought he had in him.

'We'll wait here,' said Garibaldo.

So the old priest, to show that he was well aware of the risks he was running by undertaking a descent like this at his age and that he was under no illusions about his chances of surviving the adventure, took them in his arms one by one. He murmured 'Farewell' to each of them – first Grace, then Garibaldo, then the professor – in a voice full of emotion. To Grace, he added with a return to his feisty self, 'Don't let them put a cretin in my church when I've gone.'

Then it was Matteo's turn to say goodbye to his friends one by one. He was about to ask Garibaldo to let his wife Giuliana know what he was doing, but it would have sounded insane to her, so he did not. But it was her he was thinking of as he looked for one last time at the city around him. As he lowered his head to begin the descent, and when he passed in front of the old priest to enter the tower, it was her voice he heard in his head. Giuliana had asked what no other woman would have dared ask, 'Bring me back my son.' Giuliana, who was the main reason he was here, but would never know anything about it. Giuliana, his one true love, whom life had slapped in the face. Giuliana, whose features had been obliterated by grief, but whose eyes blazed with anger. Giuliana, who said so often, wringing her hands, 'Why?' But not the way most women would have said it, in a long, useless moan. Giuliana really meant it and cursed everyone who could not reply. Giuliana, who was in him and for whom his spirit yearned.

XIV
The Gate of the Ghouls
(November 1980)

Matteo and Don Mazerotti went very carefully down the steep, irregular stairs. They hesitated at each step because there was no light. Matteo went first. He groped his way along the rocky wall, turning back regularly to make sure the priest was following him. The old man was feeling more and more ill, but did not say anything. The blood was throbbing at his temples. He had vertigo and had to cling to the rock to stop himself from falling, praying that his malaise was fleeting and that he would be able to make it down. His strength was leaving him. A new weakness was taking hold of him. He saw it as a sign that death was approaching, but he wanted to keep going to the end, to follow Matteo, to fight against the heaviness of his body and struggle on. He would die afterwards, he thought, when he had seen what there was at the end of this stairway.

After half an hour of walking down in the darkness, Matteo at last felt that he had reached the bottom, which seemed to be a cavern. A pale light floated everywhere. Not enough to see exactly where they were but enough to make out certain aspects of the space.

The two men paused to draw breath. Neither of them had any desire to talk. They did not know where they were, or what lay ahead of them, or even if they had definitely decided to continue … They were overawed. The priest took some time to get his breath back – and, for a long while, the sound of his breathing was all that could be heard, punctuated only by the crystalline ring of a drop of water landing on the floor.

They began to walk forward into what very quickly revealed itself to be a sort of labyrinth. The chambers – very small and low – all led off each other. There were numerous paths. Each chamber had two or three exits. They felt they should not try to make sense of the succession of chambers but just keep moving forward. They decided that chance would be their guide. It was possible that they would get lost, just as it was possible that they would end up in the same place whichever path they took.

Mazerotti's condition seemed to worsen. Several times Matteo had to stop to collect some of the icy water running down the walls and bring it to the old man's lips. That did refresh him for a moment but very soon his throat was on fire again and the whistling in his breathing returned.

After some hours of difficult walking, Matteo stopped dead. He put his head through one more doorway, expecting to enter a new chamber just like the ones before, but what he was now looking at left him open-mouthed with wonder. He called the priest to show him. They had come to the threshold of a room so vast they could not see the walls, nor how high it was. The immense grotto stretched out in front of them. It was covered with a sort of dense scrub. Thick bushes as tall as a man had grown up out of the rock floor.

'It's the Wailing Wood,' murmured Don Mazerotti, taken aback by his own words. He did not know how he was so certain. He knew he had never read anything about this wood, nor seen any illustration representing it, but he had spoken without a shadow of doubt, and he went on to explain to Matteo things that moments before he had known nothing about.

'This is the last obstacle designed to deter or frighten unwelcome visitors.' Then, shaken by a fit of trembling which left him pale and exhausted, he said, 'I'm not sure I can continue.'

Matteo said nothing, but he pulled the priest towards him, holding him tightly. There was no question of him continuing on his own. He would not be separated from the priest. They set off again, hobbling along slowly, and approached the wood.

Up close the trees were even more sinister than from afar. They had knotty branches with thousands of thorns, and grey flowers like thistles. They were all intertwined, which made it impossible to pass between them.

As soon as the two men approached and tried to go through, the trees moved imperceptibly, as if shivering with surprise or shaken by a light wind. Matteo and Mazerotti walked where they could, protecting their faces from the thousands of little thorn cuts that resulted when they tried to force their way through. There were narrow paths to follow but as the trees moved, they scratched their legs. It grew very dark. Soon the vegetation had formed a roof of thorns over their heads. They were at the heart of a forest that seemed to be alive.

That was when the first cries rang out, at first far off like the groans of the dying, then closer and more menacing. The forest now moved like a sea swelling at the approach of a squall. The movement of the trees was more marked, and more turbulent as well. They could feel them coming. Instinctively they ducked, but it was no use. Shadows swooped down on them. Some buzzed about their ears like carnivorous flies, others struck them on the head like angry birds. As they brushed past they took on the appearance of terrible ghouls, gargoyles wizened by time, then they took on their vaporous form again, turning in the air before swooping on the visitors once more. Their cries hurt the men's eardrums. They were animal cries, like the sound of a lowing cow mixed with a shrieking hyena. They tried to bite and scratch, circling them endlessly. They had no body and could not inflict any wounds but their throbbing hatred was terrifying. Soon, there were hundreds of shadows pressing about Matteo and the priest like a swarm of bees, coming and going and never letting go of their prey.

The priest stumbled. He had run out of energy. The harassment of the shadows had exhausted him. Matteo yelled at him in rage, trying to be heard over the humming that was all around, 'We must see it through to the end, Don Mazerotti. Right to the end!' They struggled on, leaning against each other like two blind men in a crowd.

Gradually the ghouls lessened in number and their cries grew weaker. They were letting go and it was as if the sheer determination to carry on finally freed Matteo and Mazerotti from their clutches.

They did not stop to rest immediately, certain that, if they did so, they would never find the strength to set off again. Walking on with the dragging footsteps of the wounded, they finally emerged from the forest. They fell to the ground, exhausted, feeling relieved but terrified. In front of them giant double doors rose up. They were more than thirty feet high, black and heavy as time. On both bronze doors hundreds of faces disfigured by suffering and horror had been sculpted. The sculptures resembled the shadows who had chased them. As if the bronze had taken them captive, their toothless mouths forever laughing, dribbling, shrieking with rage and pain. One-eyed faces and twisted jaws. Horned skulls and snake tongues. All these heads, piled one on top of the other in a horrible jumble of teeth and scales, seemed to eye up the visitor, warning him not to come a step closer. These were the doors not to be opened, the doors to the Underworld, which only the dead can access. Matteo and Mazerotti had arrived at the threshold of the two worlds and their exhausted bodies seemed powerless in the face of the monstrous bronze barrier.

Suddenly Mazerotti slid to the ground. He had got up to look at the door more closely, to put his hands on the sculptures in order to admire the handiwork and to try and see if there was a lock or a way of opening the doors, but he had failed. Now he lay on the ground, his hand on his chest. He was fighting with all his strength against the pain that was stiffening his limbs and preventing him from breathing, but he understood that it was time to give in. Matteo hurried over to him and took Mazerotti's head in his hands. First, he talked to him gently, then, seeing that the old man was barely listening to him, he spoke louder. Don Mazerotti's face was grey and his lips white. He could no longer feel Matteo's hands nor hear his words. His eyes stared into the void as if he saw the shadows dancing. He murmured something so quietly that, even bending over him, Matteo could not make out if he was praying or giving last instructions. There seemed to be frost in the air. Matteo desperately sought a way to help his companion, to give him his strength back – but he did not know what to do. So he talked. He begged the old man to hold on. He demanded it fiercely. 'You have to get up, Don Mazerotti. Come on! Do you hear me?' His voice was lost in the icy air. 'Don Mazerotti, hold on. I'm going to stay here. Look at me. You must hold on.' And the old man winked to show that he could hear but was too weak to reply. 'Don Mazerotti, we're going to start walking again. We have to go in,' Matteo continued but, suddenly, a strange smile passed over the lips of the priest and, gathering all his strength, he clenched his fists, saying, in a hollow voice, 'Follow me,' then he threw his head back in a death rattle and died. Matteo froze. He saw the priest's body sag as if death were pressing down on it to extract the last drop of life and bowed his head, like a man defeated.

That was when everything began to move. A shadow hovered a few inches above the old man's body. It went over to the doors and there was the heavy sound of rusty hinges moving. Hell's gate opened. Matteo stood open-mouthed. The doors parted very slowly. The sculpted monsters seemed to come to life. They appeared to moan and gnash their teeth, greedy for the life that had just been extinguished and was soon to be presented to them.

Matteo stood up. He wasn't thinking of anything any more. He simply knew that this was the moment and he must seize it. He followed the shadow and entered, leaving behind the body of Don Mazerotti with the strange smile still on his lips.

XV
The Land of the Dead
(November 1980)

The doors closed again. Matteo found himself looking over a huge open expanse. He was standing on a plain covered in black grass. It looked like those fields that Tuscan farmers burn in summer to fertilise them. Nothing else was growing as far as the eye could see except for that short grass, black and dry, that crackled underfoot. He could see clearly, but that was strange because there was no moon or stars to explain the luminosity.

By Matteo's side stood the shade of Don Mazerotti. He looked exactly like the priest – the same height, the same girth and the same features – but with no substance. Mazerotti's body had stayed on the other side of the gate, and it was the shade that was going where the spirits of the dead go. There was nothing else for Matteo to do but follow him. The shade would show the way and lead him into the heart of the kingdom.

They began to move forward and soon heard a distant noise like the crashing of a waterfall. Matteo advanced fearfully, looking suspiciously at everything around him. He did not want to make any noise, fearing that at any moment he would be taken by death, which he could feel everywhere, or that hideous creatures would come to scratch his face and eat the life out of him.

Suddenly the noise was deafening. They had come to the

banks of an enormous river. Matteo stopped and looked at the waters roiling in front of him. They were black like thick tar and topped with a grey foam that spurted in great tumultuous fountains several feet high. Whirlpools went by at great speed. The water swelled and spat, stirred up as if it would burst its banks, which seemed too narrow to contain its rage.

'What's that?' asked Matteo.

'The River of Tears,' replied the shadow of the priest in a voice without intonation. 'This is the place where souls are tortured. They are tossed about in all directions and they groan.'

Matteo looked more closely. In the waters, he could now indeed distinguish a multitude of shadows waving like drowning men, fighting in vain against the current. At first he had confused them with the river water, but, now that he was looking carefully, he understood that the river was in fact mainly shades: millions of them, one on top of the other, carried along by the current, continually toppled and whipped by the waters. A river of shrieking souls.

'What should we do?' asked Matteo, terrified. And Mazerotti's shade answered as Matteo feared he would, 'We have to cross.' Then as Matteo did not move, he added, 'Don't be frightened, the river will have no use for you.' So they approached, until they were right beside the river. And without a word the priest slipped into the water. Matteo heard a long groan escape the shadow of his friend. He tried to keep him in sight – like watching a piece of driftwood that a stormy sea repeatedly swallows and spits out again – but he lost him. He was already too far away. Matteo waited a little longer, then he had to force himself to get slowly into the water. Then he was bemused. The water only came up to his shoulders, but it was black and violent and spurted in great bubbles as if very angry. The rest of the river was made up of shades buffeted by the current. They were what had given the impression from afar of a river leaping to a great height. It was they who formed the whirlpools and groaned. Now that he had plunged in amongst them, he understood what they were enduring. Their cries reached him, their pleas, their pitiful complaints. During the descent in the River of Tears, the dead souls saw their whole lives pass by. Not their lives as they believed they had lived them, but their lives made ugly by the malevolence of the waters. The water kept beating them, and throwing them against rocks, and pushing their heads under the water and offering them a vision of their existence that both dismayed and perturbed them. Usually the picture it held up to them was neither totally good nor really bad, but marred by a thousand moments of doubt and meanness. Faced with these images, the souls moaned. Where they remembered having been generous, they saw themselves being petty. Moments of beauty were stained with small-mindedness. Everything became grey. The river tortured them. It didn't invent anything; it just accentuated what had been. He who, at the moment of fighting, had had a second's hesitation became a coward. He who had daydreamed about the wife of a friend saw himself as a lecherous pig. The river made their lives ugly so that the souls could leave them behind without regret. What the souls had loved became reprehensible. What they remembered with happiness now made them ashamed. Bright moments of their life became tarnished. When they got out of the river, battered by the waters, the souls were ready never to return to life again. From now on, they would be going where death took them, slowly and with their heads bowed.

As he crossed the river, Matteo could not help weeping. He cried for all these honest joyous lives, which were, all of a sudden, found to be ugly and despicable. He cried for these beings who now believed they had been vicious when they had actually been loyal. He cried for this river of torment which stole from the dead their most beautiful memories – so that they would become dull and obedient, shadows who would desire nothing and never make a fuss, who would join the immense crowd of those who were nothing any more. He cried for the cruelty of death, which deceived the souls in this way to assert its power, and to ensure there would be nothing in its endless kingdom except, as there had always been, the resigned silence of those who did not know desire, or tears or rage or light any more, and who walked without knowing where they were going, as hollow as dead trees for the wind to whistle through.

When Matteo reached the other bank, he found the shadow of Mazerotti. He seemed more delicate, afflicted by a profound sadness. The river had worked its devastating power and now the shadow gazed at the ground like a tired dog.

Suddenly, Matteo raised his head. A noise was growing louder and closer.

'Quickly,' breathed Mazerotti's shadow, 'hide,' and he dragged Matteo away from the riverbank. They hurriedly climbed a sort of little black hill made of scoria which gave way beneath their feet. Then once they were at the top, Matteo dropped to the ground to avoid being seen and looked back at the river he had just crossed.

'Take a good look,' murmured Mazerotti, in a whistling voice. 'Those are the shades who want to return to life at all costs. The ones who have resolved not to die. They run like mad to cross the river in the other direction, they charge and scream, but the soldiers of death always force them back.'

Straight away Matteo saw shades streaming everywhere, like a chaotic army giving charge. They advanced, impatient to plunge into the river, to cross it and to walk again in the land of the living. But silhouettes as black as quartz stood in their way. These skeletal giants threw out their arms and intercepted the fleeing shades. They caught them like you catch leaves, in great armfuls, and pushed them back without difficulty.

'There are two sorts of dead who keep trying to get back

across the river,' commented the priest in a low voice. 'The first are the shadows of stillborn babies. They haven't had any life, have passed directly from their mother's womb to the parched lands of the Underworld. They congregate on the banks of the river like insects drawn to the light. They want to live, if only for a few hours. But the soldiers of death continually push them away from the river.'

'And the other kind?' asked Matteo.

'They are the ones who have suffered a violent death, snatched from life in a second because of an accident or a crime when they still had so much to accomplish. These are the most courageous, and the most determined. They never give up and eternally try their luck. They are intent on finishing what they left behind and picking up their life from the moment it was taken from them. They left without being able to say goodbye to those they loved, and they burn with rage for all eternity.'

'So,' said Matteo, his throat tight, 'Pippo must be among them.'

'No,' replied Mazerotti, 'your son did die in an accident, but he had not yet decided what his life would be like.'

'So he's with the stillborn souls?' asked Matteo.

'He's not there either,' Mazerotti answered.

Matteo looked in the direction of the hill of stillborn souls. He saw a crest covered with shadows, little fearful shadows, huddling together as if to keep warm. As he looked more closely he saw that the children's eyes were sealed and their mouths sewn shut. They could not see anything and did not cry out. Some had died in the warmth of their mothers' wombs, victims of a ruptured placenta or poisoning, or strangled by a twisted umbilical cord. Others had had time to feel the body that housed them moan, and for the light of life to pierce their eyelids; they had cried, waved their arms, and then the flame of life had suddenly gone out and they had become still and pale like dead kittens.

On their hill they were piled on top of each other, did not understand where they were and were only dimly aware of the presence of others like them – and that was the only comfort available to them in their world of obscure terrors.

Matteo turned away. He couldn't bear to look. The fate of these beings who would never know life, who would never have the chance to love or to hate, who were dead before they were fully formed, broke his heart. Life had aborted them and no one could look at them without trembling because how could it possibly make any sense?

'If you want to find your son,' said Don Mazerotti – his voice jolting Matteo from his sadness – 'you have to go into the heart of the kingdom, where the dead are packed together.'

'I'll follow you,' replied Matteo. And they set off, leaving behind them the horrible game of the shades who were always trying to flee, and the guards who always succeeded in thwarting them – without a single shade ever, since the beginning of time, having succeeded in escaping from the Underworld.

Mazerotti's shadow led Matteo as far as a tall rocky outcrop. A massive entrance had been dug like the door to a mine or the opening to a troglodyte cave. In front of the mountain, all around the door, a wall of tall thorny bushes blocked their path.

'We have to go through,' said the shadow.

'What is it?' asked Matteo.

'The Bleeding Bushes,' replied the priest.

Matteo had now managed to get so close to the bushes that he could plainly see the tangle of thorns and knotty trunks. He stepped forward to find a way in and the branches scratched his skin. His face, legs and chest were covered in tiny cuts. He tried twisting his body to avoid injury but it was impossible to pass through without getting scratched. Here and there strips of red flesh hung down, still dripping blood onto the ground. Matteo looked at them, horrified.

'They are scraps of flesh from the living,' Mazerotti's shadow told him.

'Other living people have been here before me?' asked Matteo.

'No, but everyone who dies brings with them little pieces of the people who were closest to them. The father who has lost his son, the widowed wife, the person who has outlived all his friends. The dead person advances into the Underworld dragging bits of them behind him. But these little pieces of living people, these bloody scraps, are not permitted to penetrate any further into the kingdom of the dead. The barrier of bushes catches hold of them and they stay here for all eternity.'

Matteo looked around him. The bushes surrounding them were full of little pieces of meat. They hung pathetically, like offerings for a cannibal god or the stinking remains of a slaughter. So this was where the parts of people overcome by grief ended up. There must be parts of him here, and of Giuliana. The parts of them that had followed Pippo into death. He had to make a great effort not to throw up, and to stay strong. Then, having decided to press on regardless, he crossed angrily through the thorny barrier, letting the brambles gash his skin. When he had broken free of the dense vegetation, he gave a cry of relief and entered a vast chamber carved out of the rock.

He was surprised by the silence that reigned there. It felt as if a strange force had extinguished all noise. Not a creak, not a step, not even the sound of an insect could be heard. Little by little Matteo felt tingling in his fingers. His stomach knotted and he began to sweat. He was frightened. A visceral fear rose in him. His limbs trembled uncontrollably. A cold sweat broke out on his brow and he began to have difficulty breathing. Finally he murmured to the shadow, 'I have to get out of here or I'll scream.'

The shadow came close, and spoke into his ear so that gradually his fear left him.

'We are crossing the empty rooms that await the dead still to come. That's why you are frightened. The walls feel our presence and are seething with impatience. These enormous chambers will soon be full. Here is where the generation that was born in your lifetime will come. The territory of the Underworld is always increasing. There are more and more rooms. Huge deep chambers to cram in the corpses of tomorrow. The silence around us that fills you with fear is the silence of waiting. The stone is anxious to welcome its visitors.'

Matteo looked into the distance. There was light coming from the back of the immense hall. He felt relieved to see light and started walking.

'What is that over there?' he asked. And, since the priest did not reply, he quickened his pace to get to the back of the room. When he was nearer, he realised the room extended into a sort of terrace. Matteo approached. The terrace overlooked a huge valley in semi-darkness. He went forward to look out over the valley. The landscape was hideous. The ground seemed ravaged as if it had a skin disease. It was grey and mottled. Although dry and cracked in parts, it also spewed out putrid mud in other places. Nothing was growing except for twisted leafless trees. Matteo saw two streams which appeared to pour down the steep slopes before petering out in the valley. The first was infested with hundreds of millions of insects which formed a throbbing cloud on its surface. In the other one, despite the slope, the water was motionless. With no current, and not the tiniest wave, the water simply stagnated there for millions of years amid the stench of sludge.

Far off in the centre of the valley, on a promontory that seemed to be a mountain of coal, stood a town. It had the austere air of a citadel that time had forgotten. There were no inhabitants and no noise came from it. Tall palaces as dark as soot could be seen. There were streets, squares, terraces and gardens, but all were empty. Even the wind did not venture down the maze of little streets.

'It's the Citadel of the Dead,' said the priest's shadow.

'But where is it?' asked Matteo, a new curiosity in his voice.

'Where is what?'

'Death.'

'All around you,' was the reply. 'In every dark recess and corner. Under every stone laid here millennia ago. In the dust that flies and in the cold that grips us. It is everywhere.'

Matteo said nothing. He was observing everything around him and what the shadow said seemed to be true. He was at the centre of death. He was breathing it, he was walking on it, he was enveloped in it. Suddenly the shadow moved and indicated that Matteo should follow him.

'Where are you going?' Matteo asked.

'Can't you hear that?' replied the priest.

Matteo listened. And then he did hear, coming from far in the distance, a muffled clamour growing louder. 'What is it?' he asked the shadow, who did not reply. Mazerotti hurried towards the noise and Matteo had to follow. He was almost sorry to leave behind the spectacle of the Citadel of the Dead, because he had found it strangely beautiful. He would long remember the sight of that city where the black marble groaned sometimes as if from the pain of an old wound or out of sheer weariness.

The hubbub grew louder and louder and now the din was unbearable. It was so loud the ground trembled under Matteo's feet. When they arrived at the top of the hill, Matteo stopped for a moment. He had never seen anything like it: down below, over a vast area, were millions and millions of shades. They were moving in spirals as if drawn by an invisible force to the centre of the space, but very, very gradually. They formed a giant procession but each shade moved so slowly that overall progress was barely perceptible. The din was from their wailing: they moaned, gnashed their teeth, called for help, screamed in terror and uttered curses.

'It's the Spiral of the Dead,' murmured Mazerotti, and, seeing that Matteo was still stunned at the sight of them, he went on, 'You asked me where the shades go. Look, this is where they all end up. When they arrive they cling to the others and take their place in the crowd. And then they advance imperceptibly to the centre. Once they reach it, they disappear for ever. The centre of the spiral is nothingness, their second death.'

'But are they really going forward?' asked Matteo, who was beginning to doubt he had actually seen them move, so completely immobile did the crowd sometimes appear.

'It's the march of the shades,' replied the priest. 'They're not all moving at the same pace. It depends how much light they have in them.'

Matteo had noticed that the spirits were of variable

incandescence. Some shone like will-o'-the-wisps, others were so pale they seemed almost transparent.

'It's the rule of the land of the dead,' continued Mazerotti. 'The spirits who are still remembered in the land of the living, whose memory is honoured, and who are wept for, are luminous. They advance towards nothingness imperceptibly. The others, the forgotten dead, are tarnished and slip quickly towards the centre of the spiral.'

Matteo looked more carefully. In the thick crowd of several million shades, he could now pick out thousands of distinctions. Some were crying and tearing at their eyes, others were smiling and kissing the ground in gratitude.

'Look at that one,' murmured the priest to Matteo, pointing at one shade. 'Her cheeks are bathed in tears but she's smiling. She has just sensed that someone living has thought of her and it's someone she would never have imagined would think of her with so much affection. Look. Others are crying and pulling their hair out because they thought their memory would be celebrated and are furious to discover that no one ever thinks of them. Neither friends nor relatives. They are empty and dull. And they become paler and paler until they are totally translucent and hurry towards the void.'

'How long does the march take?' asked Matteo.

'For the most fortunate, several lifetimes,' replied the priest. 'But some disappear in a few hours, forgotten as quickly as they died. There are hundreds of spirals like this in the Underworld. The only weapon the spirits have to slow down their progress to the void is the thoughts of the living. Each thought, however fleeting, however brief, gives them a little strength.'

The priest broke off. Then in a quiet voice he added, 'Your son is there.'

Matteo jumped. Everything he had done had been for his son. But ever since he had entered these lands where the living did not venture, what he had seen had left him so dumbfounded and seemed so strange and frightening that he could not imagine seeing his son here.

'Over there?' he asked briskly as if jolted from a dream.

'Yes,' replied the old priest. 'With the others. In the middle of the dead, pulled like them by the opposing forces of memory and oblivion. There. Right in front of you. In that crowd that is trying to resist moving forward and which fears the moment they will be nothing to anyone any more, when they will have no choice but to disappear. There, Matteo. This is what you have sought for so long. Your son, who feels your thoughts giving him strength …'

Before Mazerotti's shadow had finished speaking, Matteo hurried into the throng of shades. Nothing could possibly have held him back. His son was there, a few hundred feet away, his son who he longed to see and touch and free from this inert mass of souls condemned to oblivion.

He raced down the slope, his frenzy making him faster. He paid no attention to the fact that his footsteps were ringing out in the vast darkness, drowning out the wailing of the spirits. He was running, out of breath, looking everywhere for his son. He kept running. He did not notice that the shades, surprised at the noise, had all turned to look at him. They could not escape the force that was slowly pulling them, but their eyes opened wide, as if they wanted to consume him with their gaze. All the spirits sensed escape. A man was here who could perhaps lead them out. They wriggled with impatience and joy, like victims of a shipwreck catching sight of the ship come to save them. They held out their hands, moaning, begging and rolling their eyes, pleading to be taken from death's clutches.

Matteo stopped in his tracks. He was out of breath after running, but he was not trying to recover: in front of him, a short distance away, there was a ghost shining more brightly than the others. His back was turned, but there was no doubt at all, it was Pippo. Matteo shouted as loudly as he could. Pippo. The child turned round with the slowness of the dying. It was him. Matteo struggled not to stumble. He had not seen

146

his son since the day of the accident. The features so dear to him – the cheeks he had so often kissed, the hair he had smelt at night as the child slept – were all there, before him again. The child was pale. A black stain still marked the wound on his abdomen that had killed him. Pippo hadn't changed. He had neither aged nor withered.

At the sight of his father he opened his mouth but no sound came out. He stretched his hand towards Matteo and this simple gesture seemed to involve a superhuman effort. He was struggling against the inertia of the dead.

Matteo did not waste a second. He plunged into the crowd, sweeping aside the spirits with his arms, and made straight for his child. But, quickly, the shades regrouped around him and surrounded him. They were becoming enraged. They had a man of flesh and blood who breathed and sweated life in their midst; it was an unhoped-for opportunity to escape. They tried to hold on to him, to catch his hair, grab him by the legs and hinder his movements. They were like a crowd of beggars pleading to be taken away. It wasn't difficult for him to push them back. They had neither weight nor substance and soon he had reached his son. The child raised his arms so that he could hug him – but that was when the spirits crowded round him again. They could not do anything against a real live man, but they could push Pippo away. They all tried to take Pippo's place. He was assailed on all sides, grabbed by a thousand arms, scratched by avid nails. Matteo tried to make his body into a bulwark for the child, whom he held close to him, but the assault of the dead was never-ending and he was right in the middle of a raging crowd. He did not know what to do any more. If he lost Pippo, he was certain he would never see him again. He looked at his son's frightened face. For a second, time stood still. He was not in hell, being attacked by the dead. He had just found the son he had left behind on the pavement of that cursed street. The look of terror on the boy's face now was the same as on that day. Everything was muddled. He felt as if he were reliving the accident. For the second time his son was looking at him pleadingly. For the second time he felt powerless to help him. That appalled him. He was choking with rage. His muscles tensed. He would not fail a second time and let events unfold with horrible inevitability. He tightened his hold on Pippo's ghost, pressing him against his chest with such force that he could barely breathe and hoisted him up to his face. He could feel Pippo's curious lightness on his cheeks. He put his lips to the child's face, as if to kiss him, and slowly and delicately breathed all of him in. The ghost slipped inside him; it was like swallowing water. He had not thought about what he was doing; he had done it instinctively.

He had taken back his son and he would protect him from now on with all his body, with all the weight of his living being and with passion.

In the midst of the astounded spirits, he started running towards the hill he had come from, wildly waving his arms to part the dead. He was full of a strength he felt would never leave him. He ran and the shades chased him. They were surrounding him, buzzing about. Each one begged him to take them. They all wanted to see the light again. He ran on, concentrating on his breathing and deaf to their cries.

The shade of the priest was there, by his side. It was he who guided him to the exit. He crossed the various landscapes of misery. Along the way Matteo left traces of his footsteps, the first sign of a human being in these underground worlds. He went on, no longer looking at his surroundings. He didn't so much as glance at the interminable caves with their polluted air, nor at the thin, burnt-looking trees that grew out of the rock. He ran, convinced that he was about to escape and that his return to life was just around the corner.

A new heaviness weighed down his limbs. At first it was only a little uncomfortable and did not slow his flight. He was just a little more out of breath. He made an effort and forced himself not to slow down.

That was when he spotted the River of Tears. He flung himself into it without a moment's hesitation, letting the successive waves of dead souls with their torments and stale smell lash his face. When he reached the other side he told himself that he had succeeded. He smiled to himself. All he had to do now was find the door and he would climb up out of the Underworld with his son by his side. His body was now strangely slow. His muscles were stiff and responded less speedily. He was seizing up. His mind was still clear but his limbs seemed numbed by cold. Soon his legs would carry him no further. He fell to the ground. He looked back worriedly, but was relieved to see that there were no spirits following him. They had not been able to cross the river and had stopped on the bank of the dead, envious of the man who had escaped them and frightened by the tumultuous waves that menaced them. He was alone and tried to pull himself together calmly. The ghost of Mazerotti the priest was still there. He came over to him and asked him gently, 'What's wrong?'

'Something's wrong with me, but I don't know what it is,' he replied.

'Hurry!' murmured Mazerotti. 'Stand up! You mustn't give up!'

So Matteo gathered his failing strength and stood up. He staggered again, but managed to walk on. Running was impossible. He went forward bent double as if he were having an asthma attack. Mazerotti encouraged him to continue, to hurry – and so he walked, by sheer force of will.

When they reached the bronze doors, Matteo was surprised to find them open.

'Why did they not close behind us?' he asked the priest in a feeble voice.

'It's for me,' replied Mazerotti.

And as Matteo looked at him round-eyed, he explained, 'I'm not going to die today. The door is waiting for me to leave before closing again.'

Matteo had thousands of questions he wanted to ask. He did not understand. Had the priest known this all along? By what miracle was he to be spared death? He would have liked to rejoice with him, to thank him for acting as guide but he knew he must hurry. The most important thing was to get out. So he tried to take the final steps that separated him from the door but he couldn't move. His legs would no longer respond. He was overwhelmed by terror. He looked questioningly up at the priest. When his eyes met the priest's he understood that it was useless to fight. Mazerotti looked at him with kindness and compassion.

'So this is how it is to be?' asked Matteo. He would have liked to say more, but he didn't have the breath. He would have liked to yell, and beg, to cling on to the priest, to ask him to pull him but he wasn't strong enough any more.

Mazerotti said to him, regretfully, 'Death will not let you leave again. You stole a spirit and it claims a life in exchange.'

Matteo looked down at the ground. 'There is no way out for me,' he thought. 'Very well. I am at the corner of Vicolo della Pace and Via Forcella, in Naples, on that wretched day. I'm holding my son by the hand and it's me who takes the stray bullet. That's how I must think of it. I longed to die in his place. And that is what has happened today. I am on the pavement of Vicolo della Pace and I die in his place, under the beating sun, surrounded by the frightened cries of the passers-by. It's good. I curse that idiot death, but I bless fate for killing me and not my son.'

And then in a sort of exhausted breath, he expelled his son's ghost. For a moment they looked at each other with love. They were face to face, knowing that they would never have the pleasure of living and growing old together. There would always be one of them missing and the other would have to live with that absence. Father and son. They only ever had six years. Six years to enjoy each other, get to know each other, rub along together and to learn from each other. Six short years – and the rest, all the rest, stolen.

Matteo took Pippo's face in his hands. He hugged him tightly. He wanted him there, close to him. To be able to breathe in his hair for hours, for eternity. His son whom he would never see grow up, who was going to become a man he would not know. Would he remember his father? Not from pieced-together memories, made up of what people said about him, but a real physical memory, precise like a smell or a sound? His son. He commended him to life. Matteo was filled with melancholy. How hard it was to leave Pippo. Life tore things away all the time. He breathed in the scent of the child's hair one last time, then regretfully released him from his embrace. His strength left him. He could no longer stand. Mazerotti took Pippo by the hand and led him to the gate. They slipped out through the massive doors. Matteo watched them disappear. He did not move. There he was, drained and miserable, on his knees, emptied of life. He thought for a while that he had succeeded and that he should rejoice, but sadness overcame every part of his body and weighed him down. Would Giuliana know what he had done? Would she kiss him in her thoughts when she understood how far he had gone to fetch their son? 'Tell her,' he wanted to say to his son, but no sound came from his mouth.

He was still on his knees. His face was turned towards the door. He thought of the eternity that was now going to pass like slow torture. Here he was, the only living man amongst the dead. How long would this last? The large empty chambers would be resonating with his footsteps, his shouts and his tormented solitude. He thought of all this but he was not frightened. He had succeeded. His son was alive again. He smiled with the pallor of the feverish. Incapable of moving his hands, and crushed by a weight that bent him over like an old man, he watched the doors solemnly close, condemning him for ever.

In front of the heavy bronze door, Don Mazerotti's corpse was shaken by spasms. The body that had lain inert – cooling down like a cadaver – now gave little starts. The warmth of life had brought the colour back to his cheeks. He suddenly opened his eyes and took a breath, like a diver surfacing. His heart started beating again. The cardiac arrest had, in fact, lasted only a few seconds, but time in the Underworld does not pass at the same speed and those few seconds had been enough for the two friends to undertake their journey.

Don Mazerotti stood up straight away. He was still a little pale and his chest felt tight but he could recall perfectly what had happened on the other side of the door. He did not waste time looking for Matteo; he knew he would never see him again. But he did look around for the little boy. There he was by the bronze door. A child of six who looked terribly small compared to the height of the two sealed doors. The child had his back to him. He was kneeling down and knocking with all his might on the door so that it would open again.

Mazerotti went quietly over. The child was sobbing. He was knocking and knocking, although he had no strength left. He knocked so that the door would open and let his father through. So that they could see each other again and again. He knocked, crying, wringing his hands and making terrible faces. He did not want to stay like this. His father was there, just there, in an unreachable world. His father. He wanted him. He wanted to be held in his father's arms again. He wanted to hear his voice again. He wanted the door to open.

The priest did not have the heart to do anything. He kept his distance, dismayed by the heart-rending sight of the child railing at death. He listened to the sound of the boy's repeated knocking on the bronze, hypnotised by the obstinate plea. He heard the echo of the knocking reverberating and amplified in the labyrinths of the Hereafter. Mazerotti imagined Matteo, still kneeling there on the other side, listening out and hearing the noise. He would be in no doubt that it was his son. The muffled knocks were telling the father that his son was crying for him and would never give up on him. They were relaying his love and his desire for them to live together. Pippo was there, he was calling him. Until his knuckles bled. He was communicating the irrepressible love of a child. And the father, on the other side of the door, must be blessing each of the knocks as the most beautiful present he had ever been given.

Mazerotti let the child knock until he couldn't go on and fell backwards in the mud, drunk with fatigue. He let him knock so that Matteo would not be on his own. So that he might hear his son thanking him and crying. So that he could hear the noise of life – even though it was in pain and crying – so that he would not doubt that he had won.

Then, when Pippo finally fainted with exhaustion, the old man took him carefully in his arms, as you would pick up a relic or a sacred being, and set off on the journey home.

XVI
Naples Trembles
(November 1980)

When Matteo and Don Mazerotti disappeared into the depths of the tower, they had left Grace, Garibaldo and the professor behind on the dirty central reservation that separated the two fast-flowing lanes of traffic. Silence settled over them. How much time went by? They could not have said. Time slowed down. Everything seemed to float in the calm of darkness. At first they waited as if they were at a station or in front of an apartment building. The professor sat down at the foot of the tower, his old satchel between his legs. Garibaldo smoked a cigarette, then another one, then a third. Grace, meanwhile, paced about, trying to imagine what Matteo and Mazerotti were going through. 'Why did I not go down with them?' she thought. 'Am I not also dead inside?' She thought of her precarious life, a life of loneliness and dissatisfaction. 'We only have one life and I am a mess. A ridiculous failed monster.' She thought of how she had been mocked for years in the street, and of the names she had been called with disgust and cruelty. Only one life. And hers had been one long succession of scorn and bullying. Yet, she had not gone down with them. Something in her had made her feel that the dead were not her business. 'I like my life,' she thought, smiling sadly. 'It's ugly and smells of sweat, but I like it.' And she liked the city as well, with its long dark avenues and shadowy populace scavenging in bins. 'I belong here,' she thought and was surprised to realise that there was more life in her than she had thought. She had not gone down because, in spite of the muck which stuck to her cheeks on her nights of sin, she liked being here, a bit sad and fragile like a child made dirty by the ugliness of the world.

Minutes or hours passed and gradually they were overcome with fatigue. Garibaldo sat down, his back against the stone wall, beside the professor, and Grace lay down in the grass. The passing cars no longer made them jump. They didn't even hear them any more. A haggard man with trembling lips came up to them at one point and seemed to be about to ask them for something: money, a light, or maybe something else. But when he saw the three of them he sensed he would not get any joy, and he disappeared. Later – but when exactly? – an ambulance passed, wailing in the night, but even that did not rouse them from their torpor. They must have been asleep, although it felt more like an absence than slumber, and soon it was the middle of the night. There was silence and no cars passed any more. The city made no sound.

Suddenly they were awoken by a thud. They sat up instantly and hurried over to the door of the tower and leant over, peering into the dark staircase down which the two men had disappeared. There was a figure, seemingly encumbered, coming up. His laborious breathing could clearly be heard.

'Don Mazerotti?' murmured Grace. And her voice betrayed fear as much as joy. In reality, deep down they had all thought they would never see their friends again. They thought that Matteo and Mazerotti had disappeared for ever. This sudden apparition was rather terrifying, like the return of a ghost.

'Don Mazerotti,' repeated Garibaldo, 'is it you?'

Soon they could make out the features of the man who was

struggling to ascend. It was indeed the old priest. He was panting and his face had an unnatural pallor. When she saw him, Grace thought he must be dead, but, by some kind of trick, still walking. He had the waxy hue of a corpse, with white lips and eyes sunk into their sockets. He did not manage to walk up the last few steps and Grace didn't understand what was hampering him. Don Mazerotti opened his mouth to ask something but no sound came out. He was too weak.

'He won't make it on his own,' murmured Grace.

Garibaldo leant forward, gripped the old man's arm and pulled as hard as he could. The priest was strangely heavy. That was when the professor realised that he was carrying someone and that the weight prevented him from walking.

'Take him,' gasped the priest with his remaining strength. 'Take him for the love of God!'

Garibaldo took hold of the inert body Mazerotti held out, and went back up the stairs, making sure that Mazerotti was following him. When they were finally in the open air, he sank to the ground, exhausted. It was only then that he looked at the face of the person he was carrying. He was holding a child of about six, a little boy who seemed to be deeply asleep, but who, now that he was in the fresh air, opened his eyes – large frightened eyes. And as Garibaldo was looking at him, he let out a cry that rooted them to the spot. It was the cry of a newborn, as if air was making its way through the child's throat and lungs for the first time.

'You did it?' asked the professor, stupefied. 'I was right … A gate … it really was a gate!' he repeated like an excited child.

'Where's Matteo?' asked Grace anxiously.

The old priest did not respond to any of their questions.

He struggled to get up, and still with that corpse's pallor, his hand over his heart because he had difficulty breathing and his ribcage was hurting, he said, 'Take him. To the church. Quickly. I'll tell you everything there. But, please, hurry!' And as the little group didn't move, trying to understand what was going on, who the child was and where Matteo had gone, he added threateningly, 'It's after us, and God knows what it's going to do to catch us!'

Then, without further questions, the professor led the way. Grace helped the old man to walk and Garibaldo took the child in his arms again. He had stopped shrieking and was looking about him like a frightened animal.

They ran as fast as they could, like thieves after a heist or slaves making a bid for freedom, terrified at the thought of what was pursuing them, but giddy with their sudden freedom.

The first tremor took them by surprise as they reached Piazza Gesù Nuovo. Suddenly, the earth began to growl. The tarmac cracked. The houses shook. Things flew pell-mell off balconies – laundry, flowerpots, neon signs. It was as if a beast of monstrous proportions – a blind whale or a giant worm – were sliding under the earth and making the ground undulate. Soon the streets of Naples were filled with shouting. People woken in the middle of the night were wondering what was happening and why the walls of their bedroom were shaking. The whole city was in a panic and desperately calling out. Houses collapsed, with those inside them engulfed in falling concrete.

The little group was thrown to the ground. A few feet away, a lamp post came down on two cars, causing their windscreens to shatter. In spite of his age, it was Mazerotti who was first back up on his feet. He was fired up by the urge to fight. Nothing seemed to frighten him. He shouted at his companions still on the ground, with the calm of a captain in a storm, 'Hurry up! We have to get back to the church.'

The three friends picked themselves up and followed the old man, who was marching along at a furious pace. Their progress was difficult. Only a few streets remained for them to walk through, and, all the way, there were crowds of women yelling like Vestal Virgins after the ravages of the barbarians, and mounds of rubble blocking the way. They had to give up on Via Sebastiano, which was entirely blocked by a collapsed palazzo, and make a large detour. All the way, they were amazed by Mazerotti's energy and determination.

When they arrived, the priest made them go straight down into the crypt, just as there was another tremor. It was like being in the hold of a ship in a storm. They couldn't see anything, and all they could hear was the muffled noise of falling masonry, shouts and cracking. Outside chaos reigned, and they did not know if they would ever be able to venture from their refuge. The house opposite had collapsed, blocking the entrance to the church. They hoped the church itself would hold up so that they would not be buried under several feet of rubble.

'Whatever will be will be,' said Don Mazerotti with astonishing calm. 'But if we are to die tonight, I hope at least I will have been able to tell you what I saw.'

He fetched several candles, which he lit and placed around them. First he waited for the child, who was as tired as a newborn baby after his first feed, to be properly asleep, and then, by the light of the candles, he began his tale. He told them everything. Naples continued to be shaken by spasms and he talked for hours. When the walls of the crypt shook with another aftershock, he did not stop speaking, but instead speeded up his account to ensure they would know everything before they were buried.

They felt more than thirty aftershocks that night, short, sharp and muffled like the far-off anger of the gods. Each time, the ground shook, the walls trembled and a little plaster or marble dust fell down. Fissures zigzagged across the ceiling. Each time, they wondered if they were going to be able to hear the priest's story right to the end or whether they would be snatched away, having first been crushed by falling masonry.

Eventually Don Mazerotti fell silent. He had finished. The earth around them seemed to have found its equilibrium. Grace and Garibaldo looked grave. They thought of Matteo and the child. The professor was entranced. He looked as if he were having hallucinations. He was overjoyed at the thought that he had been right all these years. The priest's account had just washed away twenty years of mockery and insults.

Slowly they stood up, left the crypt and pushed open the heavy church door to see what remained of Naples.

They went down the steps to the square like sleepwalkers, staring wide-eyed at the world. The spectacle that greeted them was unimaginable. In a few hours, Naples had been plunged into total chaos. People had taken everything they wanted to keep out of their apartments. Fearing their houses would collapse and bury their most precious possessions, they had installed themselves on the pavements, huddled together around an old family chest, some suitcases, their pots and pans or an old armchair.

In front of the church, a young woman was holding a crystal

candelabra in her arms, as you would hold a baby. The entire city was outdoors in the dark, in the middle of the rubble and broken flowerpots. Here and there some groups had a candle. To entertain the children, old people played the accordion. Some were laughing as though it might be the last night of the world.

The four men and the child walked a little way through this topsy-turvy landscape. They instinctively knew, without having to be told, that the door to the tower, down there by the port, had been buried, that no one would ever be able to descend again and maybe it was to make sure of this that death had shaken the earth with such rage. They knew they would never tell anyone about that night. They knew that in the days to come Garibaldo would report the disappearance of Matteo, who would be for ever counted among the people killed in the earthquake. They also knew they would never say anything to the child. What child of six could hear such a story and make sense of it? They were certain that the child's memories of the Underworld would fade, and they would invent some story to explain the disappearance of his parents. They would raise him between the four of them. Garibaldo would give the boy a home with him at the café because he had the space. Grace would watch over him with the fondness of a shy aunt, but one who was ready to make great sacrifices for her nephew. As for the professor and the priest, they would be in charge of his education until he reached adulthood so that Matteo's sacrifice would not have been in vain.

They were now walking the streets of Spaccanapoli and looking at the destruction the earthquake had wrought. Although they felt that they had caused the disaster, they kept silent. They thought that the old world was dead and that they would have to accept their new lives. They would raise the child, all four, in friendship, in spite of their age and the demons they all struggled with.

Finally they joined a group in Piazza San Paolo Maggiore. They brought two benches from the church to feed the fire that was threatening to go out and settled down there, protecting the child, who had not said a word and who looked around, goggling at the world he was rediscovering, this strange world where everything was shattered and fallen down. They warmed themselves at the flames of the pyre and began to sing old Neapolitan songs with the musicians. They sang so that the music would drown out the noise of the earth and Matteo, wherever he was, would hear their distant melodies. So that he would know that all was well, that they were with the child and that for Pippo life was about to begin.

XVII
My Blank Letter
(August 2002)

I stop the car at the pump and turn off the engine. A young guy comes over to fill it with petrol. I stretch my legs, breathe in the night air. There's not a pretty thing in sight. These are the outskirts of Foggia, a large, flat city at the foot of the Gargano massif: a dull suburban landscape of endless petrol stations and depressing buildings, a sprawling, ugly place with no obvious centre. I'm in the middle of nowhere and I don't know where I'm going. I'm shaky, unsure of myself, suddenly overwhelmed with tiredness. I thought my mind was firmly made up. I thought tonight was my chance and now I don't know if I can go through with it. My legs are unsteady – I'm not as strong as I thought. I can't get Grace's words out of my head. My mother. I saw the name of her village on a road sign. Cagnano. I know that's where she comes from. My hands are shaking. Have I come all this way to find her? Can I have somehow meant to drive straight to Cagnano, without admitting it to myself? No, it's my father I'm looking for. My father, and him alone.

I'm driving tonight to make up for my shortcomings. I'm going not to Cagnano but to Càlena, where the dead can hear the living. This is the place where Frederick II made his descent into the Hereafter. I'm going to Càlena to tell my father I've found the strength to look for him. It's my turn to go down and find him. I want to make up for the mistake I made the day Zio Mazerotti died. I find it hard to think about that night in January 1999. Garibaldo came to tell me the old priest was dying; it was only a matter of time. From his deathbed, he had asked for me to be woken and brought to his side. We opened the trapdoor and went down into the cellar, following the tunnel beneath the road to reach the church. The old man had not left the building in six months. Garibaldo had warned me some time before that Mazerotti's health was deteriorating and the end was near, but for days and weeks he stubbornly clung to life. A year earlier, the professor had been found dead in a car parked on the beach, stark naked, with his hands on the steering wheel and no signs of injury – as much an oddball and enigma in death as he had been throughout his life. We gave him a family burial. That was the last time I had seen the priest. He led the ceremony with the resignation and sadness of an old man weary of seeing death carrying off his loved ones but never quite making up its mind to take him.

As we entered the church, the smell hit me. I recognised it straight away: the sharp, slightly sour tang of the world below us. Zio Mazerotti had set up his bed right in the middle of the nave. The place was a total pigsty, with the shopping bags Garibaldo dropped off each morning strewn about between the pews. It had been five years since the church served any official purpose. Mazerotti no longer had the will or the energy to lead any kind of service and the Vatican had decided the church should undergo extensive renovations. Garibaldo often said this was what saved Zio Mazerotti – he would definitely have ended up being thrown out otherwise. Instead, in some faraway office, a faceless official had decided that Santa Maria del Purgatorio was to be restored, and that sealed it. The builders came to cover the façade with scaffolding and were never seen again. Some said Naples had come to the old priest's aid with the miracle of its sluggishness. The works never resumed and Mazerotti was able to arrange things as he pleased. A large black wooden bed took centre stage. Books were scattered over the marble flags and the only lighting came from candles.

As soon as I saw him, I knew he really was dying. His body was reduced to skin and bone and his strength was fading. He was as skinny as the strays that wandered the port, the dirty sheets he lay in were the same yellowish colour as his skin, and his glassy eyes seemed to be searching for invisible shadows. He was gasping for air. As I drew closer, he gestured to Garibaldo to prop him up slightly, and asked him to tell me everything. Grace lowered her eyes to hide her tears as Garibaldo began to speak. Choosing his words carefully but leaving nothing out, he told me the truth he had kept from me for so many years. I felt a huge sense of relief. I wasn't crazy after all. I really did remember the Underworld. I hadn't just been seeing things. For years, my sleep had been disturbed by cries and visions of tortured gargoyle faces. I had ended up telling myself that these were nothing but the inventions of a twisted mind, punishment for some forgotten sin. No. I really had come back from the other side. And I had passed through crowds of screaming ghosts, scratching at my face and whispering their horrible moans in my ears as I went.

When Garibaldo stopped talking, Zio Mazerotti gathered the last of his strength to tell me he was dying and if I had a message for my father, he would deliver it to him. I was stunned. Garibaldo handed me a pen and paper. Several minutes went by. Mazerotti, Grace and Garibaldo looked away so as not to put me off.

I gave the sheet of paper to Zio Mazerotti. His corpse-like arm took it and, much to my surprise, slowly tore it to pieces. 'What is empty here is full there,' he said. 'What is torn here is whole there.' I remember his commanding voice boomed around the nave, in spite of how weak he was. He asked Grace to put the pieces of the letter inside his pockets. Then he said it wouldn't be long. I didn't understand what he meant. We all looked at one another slightly questioningly, none of us knowing what to do next. When we turned back, Zio Mazerotti was dead. I looked at him. He was taking my torn-up letter with him in his pockets. What is empty here is full there. I imagined my father down there reading my letter. A letter in which I had been incapable of writing a single thing. A blank page, without so much as a signature. That was what I had given Zio Mazerotti. That was what he had taken with him to deliver proudly to my father. I couldn't do it. What could I have said? What could I possibly tell those eyes that watched me even in death, the man to whom I owed everything?

I couldn't do it, Papà; forgive me. That's why I'm driving today, heading as fast as I can towards Bari. That's why my shirt is still covered in that pig Cullaccio's blood. I've made up my mind to write that letter. It's taken me three years. I wasn't strong enough before. Forgive me. Three years. But now I'm driving. Nothing can stop me now, Papà. I'm here to show you signs of life. All my hesitations and doubts must be left behind on the forecourt in Foggia. It starts now. I've already wasted too much time.

XVIII
Alarm Bells
(December 1980)

Giuliana put her bag of shopping down on the ground in a panic. The telephone was ringing in her apartment. She felt around in her pocket for her keys. The insistent ringing commanded her to do it quickly. She felt she had to hurry as the phone call was probably from Naples.

Since the day after the earthquake, she had been trying to reach Matteo without success. She had telephoned at all hours of the day and night. No one answered. She had finally called the helpline for the families of the missing. The municipality of Naples had set up the service to help everyone who had not had news of their loved ones. On the fifth attempt she had managed to speak to someone. The man had noted Matteo's name and promised to call her back once he knew more.

It was now twelve days since the earthquake had ravaged southern Italy. Everyone had had their fill of images of the catastrophe and the ensuing misery. She, like everyone else, had looked in horrified silence at the pictures of desolation. Endless collapsed buildings and women in tears. Streets heaped up with indescribable mountains of stones and debris, as far as the eye could see. The dazed faces of policemen who did not know whom to help first. Naples was disfigured. Avellino had been reduced to a heap of dust. Giuliana had watched these images and imagined her apartment ripped apart. The walls fallen in, the floor collapsed. She imagined

Pippo's bedroom roofless, and the street below a mass of rubble, looking as if it had been hit by a bomb. She was in no doubt: this cataclysm was a new attempt to destroy her. So that nothing of her would be left at all. Her son had been killed, her love reduced to nothing, and her house and city destroyed. Every part of her had been brought down. What had she done to deserve such punishment? She did not know. She had studied the images, in silence, barely able to breathe, and it felt as if blows were raining down on her. Life was hounding her into her grave. It was tormenting her, tearing her apart and sadistically scattering the fragments. What would be left after this of Matteo and Giuliana? Nothing. Two people who had never harmed anyone and had simply tried to create a tiny bit of happiness in their little lives. Naples was dead. The city had the swollen face of a car-accident victim. Dust stuck to blood on the walls. Everything had fallen.

The telephone was still ringing. She had put her bag of shopping down abruptly and two oranges had rolled out and past the front door. She got her keys out and opened the door. But instead of rushing over to grab the receiver she stopped. The regular ringing which filled the room took her back to that morning in the Grand Hotel Santa Lucia. The same insistent ringing. The same race towards the announcement of disaster. She would run over and pick up the phone and the pain would crush her. The telephone, whether ringing from Naples to Cagnano, or in the corridors of the hotel, or in her own home, always came to devastate her life, her poor life, ever more ugly and frayed.

'Hello?'

Finally she had picked up. She sat in the armchair, still wearing her coat.

The voice at the other end of the phone spoke slowly and kindly. It asked her name. Are you Giuliana Mascheroni? Yes. And you made a request for information about Matteo De Nittis? Yes. Then there was a silence as if the man at the other end of the line was preparing himself before launching in to deliver the words she feared. He said that Matteo was on the missing list. That he had probably died on the night of 23 November when his building had collapsed in the first tremor. In any case, that was what had been reported by a man named Garibaldo, the owner of a café in the neighbourhood, who had been there at the time …

'Hello?'

Giuliana said nothing. When the man finished his explanation, he must have thought for a moment that she had hung up, because he said her name a second time. Then, when she replied distantly, 'Yes,' he said, 'I'm sorry to ask you this but what relation are you to the missing man?'

She did not reply. She had lowered her arm. The receiver on her lap continued to emit sounds: 'Signora? …' She did not hear the rest. She wearily replaced the receiver on its cradle. It was exactly the same. The Grand Hotel Santa Lucia – Pippo's death. Cagnano – Matteo's death. The telephone and the desolation that crushes you with its weight as if trying to bury you in the ground.

XIX
Càlena Abbey
(August 2002)

There's a warm breeze. I've arrived in Càlena and parked on the patch of gravel outside the abbey. It's a calm, quiet night. The wind rustles through the olive trees. The abbey stands silent and sombre. I walk around the perimeter wall. It's too high to see over into the courtyard. The thick wooden door is padlocked. It's like an abandoned fortress.

I feel a great sadness come over me. I won't scale the wall. I just want to walk. An olive grove stretches over the hillside. I sometimes think I can hear the distant sound of waves. The calm of the earth around me seeps into my veins. I'm not afraid any more. I'm not restless. I kneel at the foot of an olive tree and take out Cullaccio's other finger. I place it on Càlena's soil so that my father will feel it there and rejoice. I have brought it as a gift. Over the course of my journey, I've been desperate to get here to show him what I've done, to let him know his son has become a man prepared to take on the task of settling old scores. But now I'm here, I feel no joy. I put the finger down on the dry earth of Càlena and I know I won't be descending. I wanted to find the entrance to the Underworld, to go and find my father the way he found me. I wanted to bring him back to life, but I'm not as strong as him. I'm liable to stumble and give in to doubt. Deep inside me, there's a fear that won't go away. And so I stay here, kneeling before the abbey, and I know that for me there will be no way in. I'm not fit to confront the spirits. They would grab me, pull me towards them, consume me, and I wouldn't have the strength to stop them. I'm weak. That's how life has made me. I'm a child with a wound to the stomach, a child crying in the Underworld, terrified by everything around him. Forgive me, Father. I've come this far, but I'm not coming down. The olive trees look on with languid smiles. I'm too little and my breath is carried off on the humid air of the hills.

You're dead. I've never said that before. You're dead. I whisper it into the ground and the trees seem to quiver as if the words were tickling them gently. I thought the barrier between us was false: I was the living proof. I thought I would do for you what you did for me. It made me strong. I knew the secret of bringing back the dead.

Tonight, breathing in the sea air of Càlena, I can see it's not true. Not for me. You're dead, my father. And I will never see you again. You're the one telling me so. If it's true the dead can speak to the living, that on some nights the ground around the abbey lets a few souls come out to breathe our air or murmur age-old words to the wind, maybe it really is you telling me this. After all, where else would this feeling of calm be coming from? I'm not sorry. I'm not ashamed of my cowardice. I say I won't make the descent as if it's an order you've given me, from the depths of death. We won't see each other again. When we held one another at hell's gate, it was for the last time. I was a child then, and you squeezed me so tightly. I would have liked to show what I've become, Papà: a strong young man with big hands and a steady gaze. I wish I could have felt your arms around me one last time, but you are gone and the ground won't open up. I can feel you here in the wind and the distant lapping of the waves. The gnarly trunks of the olive trees seem to carry something of your scent. I'll stay a while longer. Is there something you want to tell me? I'm here. I'm listening. I know I'm not here for

Cullaccio's finger – that's just a miserable little lump of flesh. I came for you to tell me what you want from me. I came to be surrounded by your presence. I haven't opened the gates of Càlena, but still I feel you all around me.

Talk to me, Father, talk to me one last time. The wind has dropped. The air is still and the olive trees seem to be waiting expectantly. You're here. You're all around me. There's no anger. You're surrounding me with the warmth of your love. No one will succeed in bringing you back to life. The dead are dead and everything must stay in its place. I'm beginning to accept this. You gave me life twice and I'll give you nothing in return. I have to live. And that's all. But I can put right what has been left uncertain. I can damp down what has been left to blaze. It's what you want. I hear your whisper in the stillness of the hills. This is what you are asking me to do. It's not over. My mother. You're talking about her too. You don't use the same word as Grace, you don't say 'mother', you say 'Giuliana', and the ground shivers as if covered in goose pimples. Giuliana, and the waves surge and crash onto the shingle. I owe you this much. Everything was wrecked, but I can give you back Giuliana. My death tore you apart. She never knew you had stayed true to her wishes. She never knew you had succeeded. Bring me back my son. That's what she begged you to do. Bring me back my son. Against all logic. Because that was the wonderful thing about Giuliana: she would not give in to death, refused to be overwhelmed by grief, throwing it off like an unwanted garment. You did as she asked, but she never knew. I'm going to tell her, Father. That's what you're asking me to do. The two of you will be together again. No matter that it's too late, that the two of you have been torn apart: you'll be together. That is what remains for me to do. I'm not a courageous son. I would never have managed to descend to the kingdom below – my memories of it are terrifying enough. But you never asked me to. You just want her to know.

You're dead, Papà, but your story isn't over. Giuliana must know what you've achieved. I'll take a handful of Càlena earth with me and I'll go to her. She will love you again. She will cherish your memory. In her thoughts, she will kiss you. You went to the ends of the earth and beyond to do what she asked of you. You succeeded. And now all I have to do is show her my face to bring you back together across the years.

My mother. Giuliana. It's you I'm driving towards. It took me a while to understand. It took me a while to find your trace. Giuliana, you know nothing about any of this, cut off from the world in a dusty little village in Gargano. I can picture you dressed in black with your head bowed, talking to the shadows. I'm counting down the miles until I reach you. Soon I'll be at Vico and, from there, I'll head to Cagnano. Mamma, I'm driving towards you, and all this time you've been waiting for me without even knowing it.

XX
Giuliana's Last Curse
(December 1980)

She stood up straight on the crest of the hill. Everything around her was calm. The landscape of Gargano rustled with the busy life of insects. She knew every inch of the surrounding countryside. She breathed in deeply, and knelt down to smell the odour of pines, then she undid her blouse. The fresh air caressed her breasts. She took a small knife from her pocket. She was as pale as a woman walking to the pyre. In the silence that surrounded her with indifference, she began to talk to the stones and this was Giuliana's last curse:

'I curse myself, me, Giuliana, the woman who did not know what she loved. I believed I could make myself deaf to the world. I banished my husband, my child and my city from my thoughts. I chased away my memories when I should have cherished them as the only vestiges saved from disaster. I curse myself, me, Giuliana the ugly. I miss Matteo. I miss Matteo, swallowed up in death. I miss Pippo. My men were killed and I did nothing. I did not help them. I did not go with them. I banished them from my life. I am Giuliana the coward, who wanted to save herself from pain. So I take this knife and I cut off my breasts. I cut off the first, which suckled my son, and leave it on the stones of the hills in memory of the mother I was. I cut off the second, which my husband licked, and I leave it on the stones of the hills in memory of the lover I was. I am Giuliana the ugly; I have no breasts. I deserve nothing. Now I have decided to become old. I will be hideous and senile. I want to be a worn-out, twisted body. I will be no age. I will deteriorate quickly. I want that. In the weeks and months and years to come, I will wither. Tomorrow my hair will be white. Soon my teeth will come loose and my hands will tremble. I ask for old age and shaking. I have amputated my breasts. I am no longer a woman. No one will ask anything of me ever again. I will not recognise anyone any more. I want to be left with my memories of the past, the disarray of my spirit. I want people not to know what to do with me and to take me to a hospital where I will end my days in the solitude of failed lives. I am Giuliana the madwoman. I have decided today that my skin will become wrinkled and my hair will fall out. I will talk to myself. I will shout out to chase away the shadows that haunt me. My nights will be long with insomnia and terror that nothing will be able to cure. I am Giuliana with no breasts. I am no longer part of this world.'

XXI
The Disease that Kills the Trees
(August 2002)

I arrive in Cagnano as the first glimmers of sunlight appear. It's market day. I park at the edge of the village; I'd rather continue on foot. I look around. Everything's ugly and run down. The houses are tightly packed along a barren hillside. A barely visible sign proudly announces 'Città dell'olio', but it isn't fooling anyone. The roads are dirty, the houses empty. A mass of three- and four-storey buildings without roofs or staircases, built illegally and left unfinished, surrounds the old village. Nothing but vacant buildings. You can see the daylight through them. Who builds in Cagnano? Who are these ghost houses for? This is where my mother comes from: Cagnano, the sad face of the world.

I head further into the village and look for shops. The first I come across is a butcher's. I go in and everyone turns to look at me. I'm a stranger around here. I explain I'm looking for someone. Giuliana Mascheroni, do you know her? Giuliana Mascheroni, no? I watch their faces harden, instinctively suspicious. They reply in the negative and from their closed expressions I see I may as well stop trying. I leave and ask around elsewhere. I try other shops. Giuliana Mascheroni? I ask the kids I pass in the street. La Signora Mascheroni, no? No one answers. I slowly retrace my steps and find myself back at the market – no more than four or five carts parked in the middle of the square, all of them loaded with fruit and veg.

I watch the weathered faces of the farmers come to sell their produce. It's nothing like the pile-it-high markets in Naples – everything is counted out carefully here, as if the traders can only offer what they've salvaged from the sun.

I approach an old farmer, buy a pound of peaches and ask my question again. Giuliana Mascheroni? He stares hard at me. I get the feeling I should say more. 'I'm here on behalf of her husband. He died in Naples … I've got some things to give her … Do you know her?' He nods. Then, in thick dialect, he tells me she left years ago. Where did she go? To San Giovanni Rotondo, he replies. To the hospital. I ask if she was ill. He moves his head to say yes and no, and adds that she left to help the nurses. His wife, intrigued by our conversation, comes over to join us. 'She went mad!' she blurts out. Mad? I ask her to go on. She seems surprised I hadn't heard. She mumbles something about harming herself and a knife before the old farmer cuts in, concluding, 'The disease that kills the trees. That's what she caught.' I'm not sure I've understood. I ask him to repeat himself. 'Just like that, without warning,' he explains, 'trees can suddenly go yellow. Eaten away from the inside. Nothing to be done. The sap goes bad and poisons the leaves. It was the same for her. Just like that, without warning …'

I thank them and walk away. San Giovanni Rotondo. It's about twenty miles from here. If I leave now, I'll be there in half an hour. As I get into the car, I realise I didn't even ask the man how he knew her. I might have been speaking to one of her cousins, or a childhood friend – someone who knew her infinitely better than I ever did. But I didn't ask. I leave Cagnano and its empty buildings behind me and set off as fast as I can.

XXII
The Hospital of Suffering
(August 2002)

I stand in front of the tall façade of San Giovanni Rotondo hospital. What a grim place this is. The building's as bleak and depressing as a prison. Above the entrance, a large sign looms over passers-by, its message bearing down on them: Casa Sollievo della Sofferenza. I know those words are lies: there's no 'relief of suffering' here. House of Suffering. That's what I see written above the door. House of Suffering, as if to warn that you're more likely to die here than be healed, and not before going through long periods of pain, fever and breathing difficulties. My mother's in there, behind those walls. Who knows what state she's in. I've been to the ends of the earth and I've found her here, at the House of Suffering. I know straight away I'm going to hate this place, as I already hate the whole town and the pilgrims who flock here. Everywhere you look, in every car and shop, inside every wallet, is the bearded face of the man they made a saint. This is the town of Padre Pio, the miracle-working priest who healed the sick and hid his stigmata under woollen mittens. People come from all over the region, even other parts of the country, hoping to find some trace of his person or powers within its walls. But there's nothing. House of Suffering. It's like a warning. Through that door, it's the diarrhoea and distress of cancer patients. It's the sleepless nights and sobs of those who know nothing will save them. Through that door, it's the pointless prayers of families counting their rosaries until their fingers bleed, while the dying open their eyes wide like birds and gasp for a little more air, a little more time before the end. It's coughing fits, raging fevers and endless surgical procedures, leaving pints of spent blood around the operating tables. House of Suffering. And every patient prays he'll be the one to be spared.

I glare at the façade. If it wasn't for my mother, I wouldn't go in. I'd spit on the ground and turn back. But she's in there. I know she's in there. She can't be dead. I have to finish the journey. So I take a deep breath and I force myself to go in. I don't spit on the ground or go back to my car, cursing this horrible town. I put my head down and climb the grand steps up to the hospital, passing under the threatening inscription 'Casa Sollievo della Sofferenza'. Really I'm just like every other person entering these doors, hoping to leave my pain here and go away having gained some comfort. I come with my wounds and I hope for relief. I am like them. I want to be the patient who smiles in surprise to find he has been saved, and become one of those who is miraculously cured.

XXIII
The Corridor between Us
(August 2002)

'Relationship to the patient?'

The person sitting in front of me – a gaunt-faced woman in her fifties – lays a hand on her desk and looks up, toying with a pen in her other hand.

'Her nephew,' I reply.

Why don't I tell her who I really am? I don't know. I seem to need to approach Giuliana cautiously, little by little. Or maybe I want my mother to be the first to know who I am, ahead of anybody else.

The woman, the hospital's head nurse, doesn't blink. She writes something in her file and begins to talk. I don't listen at first. I look around the dusty little office, its cramped space and dreary decor. Her monotonous drone takes the flavour out of the words, as if she were drily reciting some official statement. The words fall limply from her lips. She's talking about treatment. She's saying I shouldn't be under any illusions. That it's a matter of slowing the decline rather than really treating the disease because – and she says this twice – there is no cure. Then she uses the term 'dementia' and pauses. 'When she first came here,' she says, 'it was to offer us help. She worked as an auxiliary nurse for more than fifteen years. Then the disease took over.' I look up.

'Do you have a sense of the state in which you're going to find her?' she asks, checking I've understood the situation. Her voice is stronger and more piercing now. Her gaze is directed straight at me. I don't move. She takes my silence as a 'no' and embarks on a lengthy explanation of her patient's condition: Giuliana, my mother, began to lose her mind several years ago. The decline was unusually rapid. Short-term memory was first to be affected. Certain distant memories remain very clear, but she finds it increasingly hard to recall what she had to eat two hours ago, or even whether she's eaten at all.

The nurse continues to paint this picture of my mother, ravaged by early-onset dementia like an attack of scabies on the brain. For several weeks, she has been unable to recognise faces, even those of the auxiliary nurses she sees ten times a day; whenever one of them enters her room, she asks their name as if she'd never met them before. She's incontinent and screams a lot, alone in her room or seated at the dinner table. She's haunted by nightmares, plagued by visions of horror. It's a curious case, the nurse adds, because the patient isn't very old. She's not even sixty, but the state she's in, she could be a woman of ninety. Still fixing me with her cold little eyes, she concludes, 'The reason I'm telling you all this is to prepare you for what's coming. It's going to be hard. I don't know when you last saw your aunt, but I can tell you for certain: the person you're about to meet bears no resemblance to the woman you knew before.'

I say nothing. Should I tell her that I last saw Giuliana – Giuliana who is not my aunt, but my mother – on the day of my own death on the streets of Naples twenty-two years ago? Should I tell her that if Giuliana's gone mad, it's because of the pain of that day, which kept growing stronger until it destroyed her and everything around her, causing her to hate my father for doing nothing and hate a life that was full only of the emptiness I had left behind, and to finally tell herself that the best, or rather, the only possible thing for her to do was to bury herself away in Cagnano, the wretched village of her birth?

Giuliana could never have guessed that death was to deal her another cruel hand, slowly, sadistically eating up her mind and turning her into a demented doll. She could never have guessed her life would end here, in the dirty corridors of the geriatric department in San Giovanni Rotondo among the shuffling patients bent by loneliness, whispering at the walls and looking fearfully about them. Maybe she doesn't care. In fact I'm pretty sure she doesn't. This life or another: it's all the same to her. She died a long time before any of this began.

'You do know, don't you,' says the nurse, to really drum it home, 'the chances of her recognising you are very slim?'

I smile.

'I know,' I tell her.

Yes, slim indeed. How will she ever recognise the six-year-old boy she said goodbye to on the doorstep one morning in June 1980 after dressing him and leaving him with his father? Will she remember the last kiss she planted on my forehead after running a comb through my hair? I remember Giuliana. The mother who smiled, though her eyes said she was sorry to have to leave so early. The mother who told herself she would enjoy some quality time with her son after work to make up for the hours lost that morning – and who could never have guessed she was about to receive a phone call that would rip her life apart and send her running, chest heaving and lips white, shedding endless tears. The mother I haven't seen for twenty-two years. Giuliana, who gave up, having no doubt concluded the world was worthless and there was no longer any point in remembering faces and names. Giuliana, who wipes her mind blank every minute and registers nothing, because the only thing that really mattered to her was swept away. Giuliana, who lives in a chaotic world of nightmares and screams, lonely and frightened. I know. Giuliana. I stand up. I thank the nurse and reach over to shake her hand so that she won't feel the need to accompany me. She gives me the room number. 507. Giuliana. It's time.

XXIV
My Father Is with Me
(August 2002)

I walk along the corridor of the west wing. I hear a voice crackling through the loudspeakers positioned at various points around the building, issuing a call to prayer. All around the hospital, those who still have the strength to respond half close their eyes and whisper an Ave Maria to ease the pain of the dying. I don't stop or recite anything. I just keep on walking.

Room 507. I stop. I've arrived. Mamma, I'm here. In a few seconds I'll push open the door and see you. I try to imagine it. When I come in, you'll have your back turned to me. I'll be surprised how small the room is – a little square space, almost entirely filled by the bed. At the back of the room there will be a window looking out on the trees. All hospital rooms are the same. You'll be standing there wearing a dressing gown left undone at the waist, falling shapelessly over your hips. I'll stay quiet for a while and then I'll say 'Giuliana' softly, to catch your attention. You'll gradually turn to face me and, as you do, I'll realise you were in the middle of saying something. How long have you been standing by the window and who are you talking to? You'll try to think who I remind you of, where you know me from, to which part of your life I belong. I might say, 'I'm your son,' in a weak, almost quavering voice, as if in apology. 'I'm your son,' and I won't dare to go any further. You'll frown. You'll look doubtful. You'll concentrate hard.

Will you remember your child? Pippo, whom you thought you'd never see again, whose memory you banished.

I have my back against the wall. The door is on my right. I try to catch my breath and slowly, carefully reach for the handle.

I am dead, Giuliana, Mamma, I'm back from the dead. My father is here – I carry him within me. It's time for you to know that he came to fetch me, that he did what you begged him to do. I look like him, don't I? The same features, the shape of my face. Maybe this will be the hardest thing for you to take in. You'll wonder if it's Matteo standing in front of you, only a Matteo who stayed young. Everything will be a muddle, Mamma, but don't worry. I'm here so that you can kiss Matteo in your thoughts and let him feel, in that faraway place, that you love him again. He did what no one else would do. I am the boy who came back from the other side. You'll look at me. Mother. You won't be able to take your eyes off me and suddenly a smile will appear on your face. You'll smile a thousand-year-old smile filled with all the light of the first day on earth.

I take a last deep breath, as if preparing for a dive. I open the door to see a dazzling white light.

We three are together again. I walk with my father into the room of your insanity. My mother. He's shaking as much as I am, he who has never faltered. He's afraid. He's waited so long to see your loving face. I open the door. For a moment, Giuliana, death no longer exists. The three of us are alive again. For a few seconds, the light in this wretched space is as pure as peace. I stand in front of you, not daring to come closer. I look at you. I say, 'I'm your son.' Do you hear me? Can you understand me, though your mind has gone? You look back at me for a long time, with an odd expression on your face. I stay still. My father is waiting too. We are here. The three of us. Time seems to go on and on. Then, with the slow, graceful movements of happy days, you open your arms.

I wrote this book for my dead. The men and women who helped to make me who I am today. Who, however intimately I knew them, have passed on something of themselves to me. Some of them were family members, others friends whose paths I was lucky to cross: all form part of the long chain of those who have gone and taken a part of me with them. If I may, let me say their names: Mathias Cousin, Jean-Yves Dubois, Simone Gaudé, Serge Gaudé, Lino Fusco, Hubert Gignoux. I hope this book gives them pleasure. What is written here is alive there.